Penny Jordan has been writing for more than twenty-five years and has an outstanding record: over 165 novels published including the phenomenally successful A PERFECT FAMILY, TO LOVE, HONOUR AND BETRAY, THE PERFECT SINNER and POWER PLAY which hit *The Sunday Times* and *New York Times* bestseller lists. She says she hopes to go on writing until she has passed the 200 mark, and maybe even the 250 mark.

Penny is a member and supporter of both the Romantic Novelists' Association and the Romance Writers of America—two organisations dedicated to providing support for both published and yet-to-be published authors.

TIME FUSE

Penny Jordan

MILLS & BOON

First published in Great Britain 1985
Large Print Edition 2010
Harlequin Mills & Boon Limited,
Eton House, 18-24 Paradise Road,
Richmond, Surrey TW9 1SR

© Penny Jordan 1985

ISBN: 978 0 263 21697 4

Harlequin Mills & Boon policy is to use papers that are natural, renewable and recyclable products and made from wood grown in sustainable forests. The logging and manufacturing process conform to the legal environmental regulations of the country of origin.

Printed and bound in Great Britain
by CPI Antony Rowe, Chippenham, Wiltshire

CHAPTER ONE

SELINA glanced tensely at her watch, forcing herself to appear calm and relaxed as she linked her hands together in her lap and sat well back in her chair. It was irrational that now, when she had already expended so much mental anguish on what lay ahead, she should be suffering these second thoughts. The pros and cons had already been weighed and having been weighed had been again, and in the end, there could have been no other decision. Not to accept the opportunity fate had handed her would be tantamount to running away, and she had learned long ago during the traumatic days of her childhood that that was simply to court further pain and humiliation. No, when she had first heard about this vacancy from her present employer she had had to resist a strong compulsion to tell him that she had no desire to apply for it, but would he have understood? Might he not have started to ask questions she could not answer, and anyway, hadn't there been a stronger compulsion; a need she had thought conquered but which flourished inside her still…a desire to see and know for herself?

She trembled slightly, a tall girl with sleek blonde hair; she took after her mother in looks and her father in build. The hint of sensuality in the arrangement of her features that she had inherited from her mother often caused the freezing disdain with which she despatched her would-be lovers to come as something of a shock. They couldn't know that she used that disdain to cloak fear and pain. 'Baked Alaska' one wit had called her when she was up at Oxford; all melting sweetness on the outside and cold as ice on the inside.

Better by far to be considered cold than easy game. Her grey eyes hardened slightly, her muscles clenching. She must not think of the past now. But wasn't now exactly the time she should be thinking of it? Easy game; she could still vividly remember one of her mother's lovers describing her thus, and she herself had lived too long with the soul-searing agonies of such a label—albeit at second-hand—to be in any doubts about that.

They had not got on well, she and her mother. She was her father's child, she had once told her and ironically she had known herself unloved because of that. Doubly ironic really when one…

'Miss Thorn?' The pleasant voice of the secretary interrupted her thoughts. 'Sir Gerald is ready for you now. Won't you please come in?'

His office was everything one would expect from an eminent QC, the very air redolent almost with the smell of respectability and wealth. The palms of her hands were sweating slightly, and she wished more than anything else, at this particular moment in time that she could simply turn tail and run. Fool, fool, she derided herself… What was she doing here?

She was here because she wanted a job as Sir Gerald's PA she reminded herself as she faced her prospective employer. Tall, with a shock of white hair, the photographs she had seen of him had not done him justice. There were lines on his face that had not been put there merely by time, a warmth in his smile she had not anticipated and which left her unbalanced.

'Miss Thorn.' He reached across his desk to shake her hand and Selina had to quell a ridiculous urge to touch him. As though he sensed her hesitancy he looked at her. Forcing a smile she extended her hand. His grip was firm without dominating.

'Please sit down.'

Breathe deeply, keep calm, she admonished herself doing as he bid. It had been hard-won the elegance and grace with which she now moved. She had been a tall gangly girl, ill at ease with her own body, who had had to force herself to accept that the grooming of the mind alone was not sufficient.

Oxford had done much to change her, but some things could never be lost. She still possessed a residue of antipathy towards the male sex which could sometimes reassert itself, often at life's most awkward moments, and when it did she told herself that it was a combination of fear and pain. At university she had once been asked by a rejected lover what her hang-up was; why she insisted on remaining a virgin. She could have told him; by then she had learned enough about herself and others to analyse and study herself objectively with cool distance, but knowing herself was easier than implementing a change.

Once long ago she had dreamed of possessing an office like this for herself, of earning praise and recognition for her legal skills, but like all other daydreams it had been destroyed by reality. Foster children did not come from backgrounds wealthy enough to provide the financial backing for a legal training. It had been a hard blow to accept, but she had accepted it, and now she was here applying for a post that at least would bring her into contact with that side of the law she found most stimulating.

Her prospective employer was talking; his initial questions were simple to answer, designed to put her at her ease she suspected, and they also gave her the opportunity to study him. She did so almost dispassionately, forcing herself not to give in to the tide of emotion threatening to surge through her. What had she expected? Instant recognition? Her lips compressed. Instant rejection would have been more likely. She should not have come here; she should have obeyed her first instincts and refused even to apply for the position. Working here could only cause her the utmost anguish. How many years had she spent training and controlling the more emotional side of her nature? And here she was on the point of throwing all that effort away, and for what? She *was* here, she reminded herself firmly, and it was too late to go back. To drag her thoughts away from the pain she concentrated on the first thing in her line of vision. It was a large family photograph depicting Sir Gerald, his wife, and a collection of other adults and children.

He saw her looking at it and picked it up smiling. 'My wife gave me that as a Ruby Wedding gift.'

She thought she was going to be sick but somehow she had managed a smile, inwardly berating herself for ever laying herself open to this pain.

'No doubt if you eventually come to work for me you will meet my family. I normally work from home during the summer recess. I have a place in Dorset.'

She nodded her head, fighting to stay calm. She knew all about Sir Gerald's Dorsetshire home and his family.

'So you heard of the post through my old

friend Judge Seaton?' he was saying. 'Well, you certainly come very highly qualified... Never thought of trying for the bar yourself?'

It was a natural enough question, but it was still one that brought pain, thin colour touching delicate cheekbones as she said quietly, 'I should have loved nothing more, but there was a question of finance.'

'Of course...quite...' There was a moment's pause and then Sir Gerald was smiling again. 'We have a very busy set of chambers here, with the bulk of the work being handled by my nephew Piers Gresham—a QC like myself—one of the youngest in the country.' He said it with pride and she had an irrational surge of dislike against his unknown nephew. He went on to describe the type of work she would be involved in and asked several more questions all of which Selina was able to answer. He had not exaggerated when he said she was highly qualified— almost excessively so for the post she was applying for, but even so she knew she ought to be flattered when he said frankly, 'Well my dear, I think I'd be a fool not to snap you up straightaway, if you are in agreement?'

For a moment caution warred with emotion. She ought to refuse; it was the only sane thing to do. She had already experienced first hand the anguish that would be a part of her everyday life if she stayed but the old compulsion was too strong to resist and almost as though it was someone else speaking for her, she heard herself accepting.

'Excellent.' His smile was genuinely warm. Who looking at him could doubt that he was exactly what he seemed; a strong, compassionate man dedicated to the cause of justice?

'Marvellous. Now if you could just check through a few personal details? Your parents are dead?'

Her nails bit deeply into her palms but she barely felt the pain.

'Yes,' she agreed briefly, 'a car accident when I was eleven.'

'And after that you were brought up by foster parents?'

'I was too old for adoption.' How coolly she said it, her grey eyes calm and unshadowed. 'And you have no other family?'

How she hated the compassion thickening his

voice. She wanted to strike out at him physically but she curbed the emotion.

'None at all.' She wouldn't allow herself to think of the grandparents who might have done so much to ease the misery of her life, but who had repudiated their only daughter, too ashamed and bitter to give her and her illegitimate child any support. They were simply another link in the long chain of betrayals that began with the man who had fathered her and who had then callously and publicly spurned her mother in a blaze of publicity that had burned scars into Selina's soul that could never be erased. *This* man, she thought emotionlessly, watching him; this man who sat opposite her with a photograph of his family placed cosily on his desk; this man who represented the law of the land in its highest state; this man who had promised her foolish, greedy mother everything and who had given her nothing bar a child she did not want. No, that last was not strictly true. Her mother had wanted her initially when she had hoped to use her as her weapon in the war she was waging against her lover's wife; but it had all backfired on her and in order to get her revenge on her lover she had proclaimed their affair to the press.

Selina couldn't remember when she first realised how different she was from other children; perhaps it was when she started nursery school and men were always waiting to take her photograph, asking her to smile, but she had been about seven before the nightmare really began, when she began to learn what all the curiosity and muted whispers were about. Sometimes it seemed as though there wasn't a single person in the world who didn't know who she was. Her mother had never made any secret of it, she remembered bitterly. In those years her mother was still able to excite press interest. After all it *had* been the scandal of the year; the successful barrister, who had promised to leave his wife and family for his mistress and who had then reneged on the bargain, leaving said mistress pregnant.

It had been said in the press at the time that her pregnancy had been a deliberate ploy to break up his marriage; her mother would have been capable of that, Selina reflected, but it still took two. Even now she still bore the scars of those early years when it seemed that everyone knew her as Gerald Harvey's bastard. The illegitimacy in itself was no big deal; there were many other single-parent children at school with her. No, what had caused the bitterness to take seed and root inside her had been the inescapable knowledge that she had been rejected; that her father had chosen his other children over and above her; that even her conception had been no more than another move in a power game. If she hated her father then she despised her mother; loathed the way in those early years she herself had been paraded about as though she were some sort of freak. She could still vividly remember the headlines she had stolen into the local library to read; the sick sense of betrayal that reading them had brought her.

Financially her mother had done extremely well out of her relationship. There had been a generous lump sum payment but, as she had complained to Selina on more than one occasion, it hadn't been the same as being Gerald's wife; of enjoying the security and prestige such a role would have brought.

Her father hadn't been her mother's only lover; as an ambitious social climber, who had seen an opportunity and taken it, there had been men before him and men after. The man she had died with in the wreck of his car had just been the latest in a long list. Selina had grown up in the knowledge that sex between men and women was a bargaining counter; a weapon that both sides wielded without thought or guilt.

She had been a pawn, used ruthlessly by her mother in her campaign to reinforce her claim on her father. He had promised her mother marriage—that much had been made clear in the press, and then had rescinded that promise. She had been her mother's last-ditch attempt to sway that decision.

All her life until her mother's death she had been an object of curiosity and pity. Other children knew her story and repeated it to her with various embellishments; her progress at school had been compared with that of her father's legitimate children at the same age. Her mother's death and the consequent muddle when the overworked social worker had mistakenly given her surname as that of her mother's current lover had brought a welcome release from all the publicity.

By that time she had craved anonymity with such intensity that her foster parents had a long struggle to even converse with her in the initial stages. They had been a kind couple and with them she had found a sort of peace, but all the time she had been tense and wary, waiting for the knowing smile, the mocking words.

They had never come and she had been free to pursue her own life as her own person. Deep inside her had grown an intense need to know this man who had fathered her; a feeling that until she did so the past would continue to trap her. She had had her life all mapped out. She intended to enter the legal arena—to enter it and conquer it, she admitted. None of her father's legitimate children had followed him into the law and not even to herself was she really prepared to admit that her fierce thirst for success owed its being to a deep-rooted need to show her father and the rest of the world what she could do.

The information that her father was looking for a new PA had been a gift from fate she could not refuse, giving her as it did the opportunity she had craved for since childhood; that of observing first-hand the man who had given her life. Did he ever think of her, she wondered bitterly; when he looked at the photograph of his wife and family, did his mind stray to her? Or did he simply consider that the money he had paid her mother had absolved him from all responsibility?

She knew quite well that it was a common fantasy of illegitimate children to crave their absent father's approval and attention just as she had done, but now, confronted for the first time with the reality of that father she was surprised at how little emotion she felt. No, she amended mentally, it wasn't that she didn't feel, it was simply that as yet she was too frozen and tense to be able to analyse her feelings. He was the same as she had imagined and yet different…a human being with whom she had one of the closest blood ties that existed and yet who did not even know who she was. For one moment she was afraid she might actually break down and cry. So much for the manfriend who had once derided her as an emotional cripple. At the time she had flinched from the words, confirming as they had seemed to do the fear that had haunted her childhood; that her father had rejected her through some fault of her own; some defect in her. Now she knew enough to realise that this was a common feeling in children, but even so some of the guilt and pain still remained.

The job was hers; and from now on she would have the time and the opportunity to study him at close quarters. And when she had done so? She frowned slightly. She had not thought that far ahead. What was she expecting, she derided herself; that somehow coming to know her father would be the answer to all the deficiencies she saw in herself? Would knowing him enable her to cast aside her dread of emotional commitment in order that she could take a lover, for instance? One step at a time she told herself. One step at a time.

'Just before you leave my dear, there's someone I should like you to meet.'

For one dreadful moment Selina thought he must mean his wife; that was something she wasn't ready for—not yet—but she realised almost instantly that that was hardly likely. He reached out and pressed his intercom. 'Would you ask Mr Gresham if he could spare us a moment please, Sue?' he instructed his secretary.

'I'd like you to meet Piers before you leave,' he told Selina with a smile, 'you and he will be working quite closely together at times—as well as his own briefs, he does a great deal of work for me.' He broke off as the door was thrust open,

Selina turning automatically to witness the entrance of the man he was talking about. Tall, even taller than her father, he combined an intensely powerful sexual aura with an air of cool hauteur that Selina found instantly intimidating. It was all too easy to imagine his effect on a jury—or on a witness—and Selina shuddered finely without realising she was doing so.

Heavy eyelids lifted to reveal eyes of a startlingly deep shade of blue, which studied and dissected her with a scrutiny as powerfully honed and as icy cold as polished steel. Just the effort of holding that penetrating stare made her muscles ache with tension.

'Piers, come in and meet my new assistant.'

Sir Gerald put a friendly hand on the younger man's arm as he went forward to meet him. The family resemblance was slight, but there none the less, although Selina suspected that even in his youth her father could never have possessed the cold demeanour that was so evident in his nephew.

'Miss Thorn.' His voice was cool too, cool and deep, and just hearing it brought a rash of goosebumps up under her skin. He obviously knew about her already since he knew her name, and

Selina was annoyed to find herself almost reluctant to accept the hand he held out towards her. The touch of his fingers was warm, the sensation of his skin against her own so acute that she badly wanted to pull away. He emanated a raw sexuality that made Selina feel uncomfortable. She had come across it before, but had always shied away from such men fearing them instinctively, although she had learned to disguise her fear as contempt. She did so now, without realising what she was doing. Her eyes and mouth cold, her chin tilted at a defiant angle. The swing of her blonde hair revealed the slender length of her throat, her formal business suit emphasising the slender seductiveness of her body.

'Have we met somewhere before?'

His question over-balanced her, her eyes unknowingly widening and turning a dark smouldering grey as she was forced to look back at him.

'No…no I don't think so.' They had never met before, and he must know it so why…

Sir Gerald's laughter interrupted her worried thoughts. 'Not a very original line, Piers, although I must say I don't blame you for trying.'

Selina was pretty sure that nothing had been

further from Piers Gresham's mind than making a pass at her. She didn't normally appeal to men of his type and she had always taken care that she should not do so. It was on the tip of her tongue to suggest that what her cousin saw in her was a family likeness, but to do so would be the utmost folly. That she should consider the risk almost worthwhile simply to see the expression on his face warned her that she was reacting far too much to him.

After a few minutes brief conversation Piers Gresham left them, and once he had gone Selina found it a good deal easier to relax. Before her interview her sole worry had been that her father might somehow recognise her and she had not really thought beyond that. Now she had been made uncomfortably aware of the fact that her emotional response to her father was not going to be her only problem. Would she be able to work with Piers Gresham without allowing her sexual fear of him to surface? Men like Piers Gresham possessed a masculinity they couldn't resist reinforcing, just as her father hadn't been able to resist the temptation of her mother. It would have been easier to bear if her mother had been merely a victim in the whole shabby affair rather than a participant, but her mother herself had admitted to her that she had been determined that her lover should marry her; and that he should desert his children and divorce his wife in order to do so.

'Why not?' she had demanded of Selina, sensing her distaste. 'It's no more than many other men have done.'

Her mother had been a very selfish woman, Selina acknowledged inwardly, attractive enough to use her looks to get what she wanted from life, but on that occasion she had gambled too high and lost, and she had never let Selina forget that had she known her lover would abandon her, his child would never have been conceived. Once that had hurt, but like all the other pains she had learned to bury it; to deny it life, just as her mother would have denied her life.

She had taken the morning off from her job to go for the interview. There was no secret about it. The judge for whom she worked had encouraged her to apply for the job and had even told her about it. Judge Seaton and his wife were the only two real friends she had, Selina acknowl-

edged as she made her way back to his house.
Now semi-retired, he was collating his memoirs
and Selina had been helping him. He and his
wife had been married fifty years and still found
pleasure in one another's company. Tonight she
was going out to dinner with them to celebrate
the Judge's birthday. She wasn't particularly
looking forward to it. Susan Seaton was a
motherly woman who couldn't understand why
an attractive girl like her husband's assistant
should so consistently shun the male sex, and
Selina had long ago lost the habit of confiding
in anyone and was, therefore, unable to tell her.

The Seaton's house was in a quiet Chelsea
mews; elegant and comfortable; a true home
Selina reflected as the housekeeper let her in.

'Good, you're just in time for lunch,' her
employer exclaimed when he saw her. 'Come
and tell us all about it.'

She did so with the quiet self-control that marked
her behaviour. Susan Seaton smiled warmly at her,
marvelling at her lack of excitement. At Selina's
age she had already been a mother, but she had
never possessed this girl's cool control. Sometimes
it worried her. It was almost unnatural for a girl of

her age to be so contained. She had rarely heard her laugh or seen her cry, and she had worked for her husband for three years, living almost as closely as a member of the family.

'I never thought for a moment that Gerald would turn you down,' the Judge told her. 'He'll make use of your mind,' he warned her; 'I know he's talking about retirement, but he's still a powerhouse of activity; he's one of our foremost QCs, with young Piers looking likely to follow in his footsteps. Now there's a man to reckon with; an excellent defence counsel, but positively lethal in prosecution. He seems to possess an intuition that leads him right to a person's Achilles heel. He's as close to Sir Gerald as a son—perhaps closer; in fact I'd say after his mother his uncle is the only other person he's fond enough of to allow him to sway his judgment. Gerald stepped in and took over the role of surrogate father when his own died. His sister Dulcie was widowed very young. Piers will be taking over from his uncle when Gerald finally retires.'

'Wait until you meet him,' Susan Seaton enthused, her eyes sparkling. 'He is quite devastatingly attractive.'

'I met him today.' Selina said it quietly, her head bent over her soup plate. Over her head the older couple exchanged glances.

'You don't sound very impressed. He's a very able, almost an inspired barrister.'

'He struck me as being rather conceited and sexually domineering,' Selina said coolly, 'but it hardly matters what I think. After all we're not likely to come into much contact with one another.'

'Don't be so sure,' the Judge cautioned her. 'Gerald relies a good deal on Piers, and since he's training him to take over from him, I suspect you might find you see quite a lot of him.'

The thought was extremely unpalatable. She had disliked the man on sight, Selina admitted; something about him was as abrasive to her personality as being rubbed with sandpaper; something over and above the fact that he belonged to a type of male animal she most disliked. There had been an instant awareness between them that she couldn't deny, a look in his eyes that cautioned her to tread carefully, causing her to seethe with resentment that it should be so.

* * *

To celebrate his birthday the Judge had booked
a table at one of London's more exclusive restau-
rants. Selina left her own small flat in plenty of
time to reach the Seaton's house at the appointed
time. Her dress was a plain slip of cream silk she
had bought in Brown's sale. High-necked and
long-sleeved, she considered it a suitable addition
to her wardrobe, without realising that the silk
moved with her as she walked, caressing her
elegant body with a sensuality that very few men
could remain unaware of. She simply saw it as the
right sort of dress to wear out to dinner. She liked
good clothes and wore them well; choosing them
for elegance and wearability rather than sexual
appeal, not knowing that the body they clothed
was sexual enticement all by itself. Having taught
herself to clamp down on any sexual urges she
might feel almost from childhood, Selina was
blind to them in others. If she ever happened to
catch a man looking at her, studying her, she
would look back in an icy disdain that normally
made him retreat. The first attempt any male
escort made to touch her was always the last. Sex
was a weapon that could inflict terrible wounds
on the innocent as well as the guilty and it was

one she herself would never descend to using. She might be her mother's daughter, but she would never be branded as *she* had been. She would succeed without using her body; without betraying her principles. She had to.

The restaurant was busy; a sea of unfamiliar faces; the table to which the Seatons and Selina were shown was slightly secluded from the others.

Susan Seaton ordered her food with relish. In many ways Selina almost envied Susan. She was a happy, contented woman who had devoted her life to her husband and family and who had been repaid in turn by their love and protection.

Beyond the tables and diners there was a small dance floor. Music was provided by an immaculately dinner-suited pianist.

'My, it quite takes me back,' Susan sighed nostalgically as they waited for their food. 'Do you remember, Henry, when we used to go to the Savoy? You took me there for our first wedding anniversary.'

'And you were sick,' the Judge smiled.

'And we both thought it must have been something I'd eaten, until we discovered that I was carrying John.'

The Seatons had three children and several grandchildren. At the weekend they would be driving down to their eldest daughter's for a family celebration. Selina closed her mind against the thought of it. Family occasions were something that belonged to other people. They had no place in her life.

They were halfway through their meal when the Judge put down his knife and fork and said mildly, 'Good heavens, talk about coincidences. There's Piers Gresham.'

'Where?' His wife craned her head to look. 'Who's that with him?' she asked. 'Do you recognise her?'

The Judge shook his head. 'I've no idea who she is.'

Selina glanced up from her food and glanced briefly at the other couple—Piers Gresham was seated several tables away facing her. All she could see of his female companion was her back view, but that was enough for Selina to grimace slightly. The other woman was wearing a dress that revealed most of her tanned back; a dark fall of hair brushing her neck. She was dressed in a way designed to catch a man's eye, and as always

Selina felt her muscles tighten at the sight of such open sexuality. It offended her and she shrank from it, unaware that her distaste was mirrored in her face or that she was being observed. Her reactions to other people's sexuality always distressed Selina; she knew deep down inside herself they were a legacy from what she had endured as a child; from knowing that she was the fruit of a union that had been motivated on one side by sexual greed and on the other by social avarice but knowing the reason for her reactions did not help her to come to terms with them.

Piers Gresham had obviously seen them. When they had finished eating he came across to their table, urbane and charming as he chatted to the Judge and his wife, but his eyes were constantly assessing Selina, his scrutiny of her making her tense and uneasy.

'You and Selina met this morning, I believe,' the Judge said turning to draw her into the conversation. 'Your uncle is gaining a very valuable aide in her.'

'I'm sure he is. Perhaps you'd care to dance

with me, Selina, and we could get to know one another a little better?'

Other couples were already dancing and the Seatons obviously saw nothing untoward in the invitation because they were both smiling expectantly at her. Across the room her eyes slid to the dark-haired girl waiting at the table and a fierce surge of anger swept over her. Who did he think he was? Some sort of irresistible God who had merely to speak to have women worshipping at his feet? It didn't strike her that her reaction was wildly illogical; she was possessed by some elemental surge of emotion that warned her that this man was dangerous and to be repudiated at all costs. Without stopping to weigh her words, she said coldly, 'I'd rather not if you don't mind.' Her eyes flicked over to the girl waiting for him, and so she missed the glint of cold anger in his eyes, 'After all, our relationship *is* going to be professional rather than social, and I prefer to have things plain from the start. It makes for a much less complicated life.' She looked straight at him as she delivered her cool words, caught off-guard by the depth of anger she saw in his eyes.

'That was rather over the top wasn't it?' her employer remarked when Piers had gone.

Trying not to flush at the faint criticism in his voice Selina shrugged. 'He only asked me out of politeness. He already had someone to dance with.'

'Even so, you rejected him extremely pointedly,' the Judge told her. 'No man likes being rejected, Selina,' he told her gently, 'especially not in public. Be very careful, my dear. He could make an extremely powerful enemy.'

'Because I refused to dance with him?' Selina injected a note of acid scorn into her voice. 'Wouldn't that be rather small-minded?'

'He's a man, my dear,' the Judge told her wryly, 'and we males are notoriously vulnerable where our egos are concerned. We weren't the only ones to hear you refuse him,' he added gently, 'and you must admit that as a put down it was decidedly strong.'

Not wanting to admit even to herself that she had been betrayed into hasty speech because of her own response to his sexuality, Selina shrugged slim shoulders. 'The odd rejection does none of us any harm from time to time.' She glanced over to where Piers was now dancing with his companion, and added cynically, 'I doubt he'll lose any sleep over it. He seems more than happy with the dancing companion he's got.'

'Umm, well tread carefully,' the Judge warned her. 'He's not a man *I'd* like to get on the wrong side of.'

Instinct had already told Selina that and she couldn't understand why she had been so rude to him. There had been other men before whom she had disliked equally as much and yet she had managed to conceal it from them. Not so with this man. He had recognised her rejection for what it was; she had seen the realisation flare and burn in his eyes and she shivered sensing that there would be some form of retribution...

Whatever it was she could cope with it. She had coped with similar situations before and emerged unscathed. What she had to do now was to concentrate on getting to know her father so that she could at last free herself from the guilts of the past, because until she did they would continue to poison the present and the future.

CHAPTER TWO

SELINA'S first week in Gerald Harvey's employ passed quickly. During their interview she had been too wrought up and tense to do much more than concentrate on his questions, but now that she was settling down into the day-to-day routine she found herself watching him; wondering what he would say if he knew the truth; how he would react. She had promised herself long ago that she would never fall into the trap of wanting an emotional commitment from the man who had fathered her and all through her growing up, although she had followed his career, she had never ever allowed herself to think of him as her father—to her he had simply been her mother's lover; and then her opponent in a battle in which she herself had been used as no more than another weapon. She had never anticipated feeling any emotional response to him; after all why should she; and yet, illogically, it was there; it was disconcerting to discover how easily they meshed and at the end of the first week he turned to her and said warmly.

'Selina, I'm going to bless the day I hired you. We seem to have achieved a working rapport in a remarkable short space of time. Do you think you'll be happy with us?'

Happy? Selina tried to analyse the word. What was happiness? She had reached a goal and that in itself brought with it its own sense of achievement, but happy…

'I'm sure I shall be,' she told him equably, lowering her head so that he couldn't see her face. This man was her father; they were united by ties of blood and heritage and yet…

'Is something bothering you?'

He asked the question quietly, coming to stand immediately behind her, one hand on her arm. There was nothing sexual in his touch; it was merely concern, and Selina was shaken to discover that tears were pricking her eyes.

A sound outside her vision broke the silence between them. Someone had opened the door, and Selina felt her nerves curl in bitter tension as she heard her father say genially, 'Piers, it's good to have you back. Did all go well?'

It had been a relief to Selina to discover that Piers Gresham was away for several days. He had gone to stay with his godfather, Sue, Gerald's secretary, had told her. But now he was back.

'Fine.'

Selina could feel the intensity of his gaze concentrated on her, forcing her to lift her head. Something in her eyes made his narrow and sharpen, moving from her face to her father's and then back to hers again, his mouth grim. Sue ran through to advise her father that she had a call waiting on the line for him and as both she and Piers moved away out of earshot Selina was stunned to hear him say warningly.

'I don't know what game you're playing with my uncle but it better not be the one I think it is. He is a married man you know, or is that what you prefer? If so, you won't find him any pushover, he was nearly caught that way once before.'

Sick to her stomach Selina stumbled past him, making for the sanctuary of the Ladies' cloakroom. Once inside she was furious with herself for the nausea that choked her throat. What was wrong with her? She had only herself to blame for Piers' hostility. But that was no reason for him to assume that simply because his uncle was touching her arm that she had deliberately… Her stomach lurched. The man was her father for God's sake. But *he* did not know that and neither did Piers Gresham.

It was a good fifteen minutes before she felt in control enough to leave the Ladies. On her way back to her office she passed Sue. The other girl gave her a curious glance. Sue had a boyfriend with whom she lived and to whom she was devoted. That did not stop her from flirting with every male who crossed her path, though. However, she was a good-natured girl, as warm and open as she herself was silent and reserved Selina acknowledged, returning her smile.

'You okay?'

'Fine. Is Sir Gerald off the phone?'

When Sue nodded Selina opened the door and walked into her father's room, but it was Piers who stood behind the desk not her father. She came to a full stop, aware that the tiny hairs at the back of her neck were raised in primaeval awareness.

'Excuse me.' Her voice sounded artificially polite. 'I was looking for Sir Gerald.'

'He's just popped out. Don't run away, I'd like to talk to you.' As he spoke he put down the brief he had been reading and came towards her. A panicky desire to turn and flee almost over-whelmed her, but Selina withstood it. She was going to have to accustom herself to this man's presence; after all they would be working in the same set of chambers; they were bound to meet occasionally and the sooner she learned not to react so intensely to him the better it would be.

'What made you apply for this post?'

His question caught her off-guard. For a moment she said nothing and then stammered. 'I…I…I was ready for a change,' she managed at last.

'Is that so? You know you're remarkably well qualified for a young lady who is content to be merely a PA. Have you never thought of taking on something more challenging? You have an excellent degree.'

'I have my ambitions yes.' Selina tried to mimic his cool self-possession.

'And what are they, I wonder?' He was coming towards her now, stalking her almost, she thought angrily. What was he hoping to achieve? 'My uncle thinks very highly of you. In fact I'd say he's taken to you in a remarkably short space of time. Most unusual. He's normally a very cautious man where attractive young women are concerned.'

'Why?' Selina asked flippantly. 'Does he have a jealous wife?'

Just for a second she was alarmed by the gleam in the midnight blue eyes, but then it was gone, his expression flat and unreadable.

'Not very clever, Miss Thorn,' he said at last. 'If you're only half as clever as I think you are you must have read all there is to read on my uncle; done all your background research before you applied for this job. You know very well why he would want to avoid any sort of entanglement outside his marriage don't you?'

Selina felt as though the floor had suddenly dropped away beneath her, leaving her on thin ice.

'I know that many years ago your uncle was involved with another woman,' she agreed coolly, turning aside with what she hoped was a calm disdain as she added, 'but then so have many other prominent men.'

'Indeed they have, but very few have attracted the subsequent blaze of publicity and notoriety suffered by my uncle. I was eight years old at the time. My aunt almost suffered a nervous breakdown.'

'I'm sure it must have been an extremely traumatic time for you all.' Selina was distant, her voice clipped. Don't tell me any more, it warned him, I don't want to hear, but her warning signals were ignored.

'My uncle has three daughters; the eldest one was expecting her first child at that time; she lost it; the second ran away from school because she could not endure the torment inflicted on her by her schoolmates. You're looking quite pale, Miss Thorn. Do you find what I'm relating to you upsetting?'

'It was all a long time ago,' she managed to say, hating him now with an intensity that made her long to physically assault him. How dared he tell her all this…. Didn't he think that *she* had suffered…that she… She pulled herself together before she lost control completely.

'I can assure you that I have no desire to break up your uncle's marriage,' she told him crisply. That much at least was true.

'Maybe not,' he agreed slowly, 'but you have *some* ulterior means for being here. I can sense it. Body signals are a very strange thing, Miss Thorn,' he added watching her. 'They give away to others so much more than we want them to see. Why do you dislike me so much?'

'How could I dislike you? I barely know you.' Selina forced a cool smile, 'I think you're suffering from an ego problem, Mr Gresham. I am merely indifferent to you.' She was lying and she suspected that he knew it but she wasn't going to back down.

'Is that a fact.' He said it softly closing the distance between them before she could move. 'Well, let's just find out how much truth there is in that statement shall we?'

The hard warmth of his mouth as it covered hers shocked her into submission. She could feel the steady beat of his heart against her body, but her own refused to mirror its firm rhythm. It thudded threadily, her body tensing in mingled shock and rejection, her eyes blazing bitter defiance and fury as she fought against the domination of his hands and mouth. He was kissing her with ruthless precision and a great deal of sexual expertise; her body shamingly recognised that, even while her mind was disgusted by it. As soon as he released her Selina slapped him, panting hard as she delivered the hard blow.

It left the palm of her hand smarting and a white welt of flesh against his lean cheek which was now slowly filling with dark blood.

'Don't worry, I'm not going to repeat the experiment.' For some reason his soft words brought darting flares of pain. He watched her, eyes slitted, 'Do you know,' he added, 'I've always considered that that particular form of retaliation sprang more from sexual frustration than annoyance. Perhaps sometime it might be worth while putting my theory to the test.'

The way he said it made her blood run through her veins in angry fire. 'Not with me you don't,' Selina told him rashly.

For a moment something came and then went in his eyes and when he spoke again, he appeared totally in control, unlike her, Selina reflected bitterly as he drawled. 'Well now a man with an ego like mine just might consider that challenge to be an invitation, my dear. Is that what turns you on? To slap a man down and then needle him into physical savagery? If so, it's a dangerous hobby.'

She wanted to spit and fly at him like an angry cat. No one had ever tossed such outrageous accusations at her before, and certainly not in a languid, almost soft voice that suggested that there was no possible way in which its owner's assessment of her could be wrong.

If her father hadn't walked back into his office just then Selina didn't know how she would have reacted. As it was she muttered something about a phone call and excused herself. It was only later, safe in her own flat, that she was forced to admit to herself that resent it though she did, Piers Gresham had managed to provoke a physical response from her in a way that no man had done before. Even now she found it impossible to accept that there had been that moment of fierce need to respond to his kiss; that sensation of melting and then burning that urged her to yield. But she hadn't done so. He had broken the kiss before she had betrayed herself that much.

From the first moment she saw him she had known that Piers Gresham was a man to be wary of. Now this impression had been reinforced a thousandfold. It would be a long time before she forgot how he had looked at her when he questioned her. So he didn't trust her did he; well she didn't trust him either.

Back in her flat that evening some impulse she couldn't contain led her to study her features carefully in her bedroom mirror. What had Piers seen there that had led him to make his accusations? A formidable man the Judge had called him; for formidable she would have said diabolical Selina thought mentally. Even now hours after her encounter with him her pulses still fluttered at the thought of him, her mind and body unable to relax from the turmoil he had caused, and she for the space of one heartbeat had been in real danger of succumbing to him, of forgetting everything she had learned during her life and responding to his kiss... It would never happen again. Maybe the Judge had been right and she had been wrong to react as she had done in the restaurant, but even then her body had been sending her signals that had terrified her and she had reacted instinctively, too frightened by them to use reason and logic.

For some reason that evening she found it impossible to settle. Normally she enjoyed the quiet hours of solitude in her flat. After the hectic bustle of her foster parents home, where, despite their kindness, she had never felt she fitted in, she had come to relish the peace and quiet of her own home. The books she had collected at Oxford lined her bookshelves; the antique dresser she had found at a country market and lovingly restored holding her china and few little treasures. Her flat was in a large old house with a pleasant garden which she shared with the other tenants, most of whom she knew to say good morning to but very little else. That was the way she had wanted her life, free of complications; of people who might ask questions and force her to lie.

At university she had dreamed that somehow she might be able to follow in her father's footsteps, but of course it had been impossible. One needed financial backing to train as a barrister, something she did not have, and although her tutor had suggested a legal career in industry she had not been interested. Without a proper legal training she would always have remained in a junior position in a large department. That wasn't what she wanted. The law courts, the Inns of Temple, the measured, controlled world of the law; that was where she had set her sights. That was why she had settled for jobs for which she was desperately over-qualified because at least then she was breathing in the atmosphere she craved.

All through her teens she had been consumed by a desperate need to prove to the father who had rejected her what he lost in doing so. As she grew older those dreams had faded, reality taking their place, and yet she had no more been able to resist the temptation to apply for her present job, knowing it would bring her into close contact with her father, than she had been able to resist Piers' kiss.

Working closely with her father was a bitter-sweet experience. She had long ago abandoned her adolescent dreams of winning his admiration and love and even her resentment over the way she had been rejected had eased, but there was still a measure of pain in seeing and knowing him when he did not know her.

She was glad of the weekend, because it gave her time to relax and unwind, but on Sunday morning when Susan Seaton rang and invited her over for lunch, Selina was ready to admit that for once she had had enough of her own company.

As she had half-anticipated the Seatons had several other guests. Susan Seaton, used to the demands of a large family, enjoyed entertaining, and Selina found herself chatting to an attractive older woman who also appeared to be on her own.

'Since Susan is too busy to introduce us, we had better perform that task for ourselves. I'm Dulcie Gresham,' she told Selina.

With a small start of shock, Selina acknowledged the introduction. 'Selina Thorn,' she told her companion, suddenly wishing she was talking to anyone other than this woman. Now that she knew her name it was impossible not to recognise her as Piers' mother. It was from her that he had inherited his dark hair and his navy-blue eyes, although in his mother they were softer, more compassionate.

'Goodness, what a coincidence,' she exclaimed warmly, 'You're my brother's new PA, aren't you? But then of course, not so much of a coincidence really is it, because the legal world is a very close-knit one and of course, you did work for the Judge previously. How are you enjoying working for Gerald, or would you rather not say?'

'I'm enjoying it,' Selina told her truthfully. 'It's very different from working for the Judge of course, but then I was ready for a change.'

'Yes, my son tells me you're extremely highly qualified. Have you never thought of the bar as a career for yourself?'

His looks weren't the only thing he had inherited from his mother Selina thought wryly. Although it was less abrasive in Dulcie Gresham, Selina could see where her son got his sharp intelligence from.

Almost as though she sensed her hesitation her interrogator's manner softened, a wry smile curving her mouth. 'Forgive me, I'm afraid at times I do sound rather like the cross examination. Years of living with lawyers I'm afraid. My late husband was a barrister as well. In fact I should very much have liked a career at the bar myself—I find it fascinating even now, but of course in those days…'

Charmed against her will Selina heard herself admitting. 'I should have liked to make a career in law, but after university there just weren't the funds.'

Her companion's expression was instantly apologetic. 'My dear, how crass of me, I am sorry. Of course, it is an expensive career to train for, but you are enjoying working as my brother's PA. His chambers have an excellent reputation and you will find yourself involved in all manner of fascinating cases I am sure. How did you get to hear about the job? I didn't think Gerald intended to advertise it until later in the year. He suffered a slight heart attack just before Christmas you know and Mary, his wife, and I prevailed upon him with my son's assistance to get himself some more help at the office.'

Was she being subjected to a subtle investigation Selina wondered? But no, she was being unduly suspicious. Even if Piers Gresham had confided to his mother his suspicions of her, it was taking coincidence too far to believe that the older woman had come to this luncheon partly purely to question her.

'The Judge mentioned it,' Selina said truthfully. 'He knows of my fascination with that side of the law, and he thought it might be an ideal position for me.' What she couldn't say was the heart-searching she had endured just after the Judge had dropped his bombshell. Here it was, being dropped right into her lap; just the sort of opportunity she had dreamed about as an adolescent. The chance to meet and get to know her father. However, her own strong moral code had made her question the wisdom of trying for the job. If her identity was discovered it would lead to unpleasantness; working for her father was probably only likely to cause heartache to herself as well.

She had long ago abandoned her childhood fantasies of a loving, caring father, and yet the reality of working for him, knowing that he was sublimely indifferent to her existence might be more than she could cope with. In the end, though, the temptation had proved too great, and she had not been able to resist.

'I'm sorry.' Selina came out of her reverie to realise that her company had been saying something, and that she was now regarding her with a faintly quizzical expression. 'I'm sorry,' she apologised again, colouring faintly. 'I'm afraid, I didn't...'

'I was just remarking that Harry Frobisher is looking over this way rather a lot. Do you know him?'

Harold Frobisher was a young solicitor whose father had been a friend of the Judge's. Selina didn't particularly like him. He was a slick, sharp young man who was overfond of touching her when she would have preferred him not to.

'Slightly.' Her response was guarded and again Dulcie Gresham smiled. 'I quite agree,' she said lightly. 'Not a particularly attractive young man. Do you have a boyfriend, Selina? I may call you Selina, mayn't I?'

'Please do. No…not at the moment.'

'Very wise. A pretty girl like you should take her time before deciding to settle down.'

Selina saw the Seatons making their way towards them and smiled warmly, unaware that Dulcie Gresham was watching her until she said in a thoughtful voice. 'Do you know, Selina, you remind me of someone, but I cannot for the life of me think who it is.'

Selina was glad that she was looking away, otherwise she might have betrayed herself completely. Cold fingers of fear clutched at her heart. Dear God, don't let her realise the truth, she prayed… She couldn't bear to be revealed here, publicly, before the Seatons whom she respected and liked so much, as the daughter of the woman who had caused so great a scandal in their small circle.

For once fate seemed to be on her side. The Seatons reached them, Susan hugging her warmly while the Judge kissed Dulcie's cheek.

'I can see that you've introduced yourselves to each other. I take it that Piers couldn't make it, Dulcie?' Susan released Selina to question her friend.

'Other commitments I'm afraid,' Dulcie confirmed. 'But he does send his apologies and he will be calling to collect me later. An urgent brief that needed studying.'

'Yes, it will be the Mountford case,' the Judge interrupted. 'I heard they wanted him for that. Unusual for him to take on a divorce though, isn't it?'

'He and John Mountford were at school together, and there's rather a lot of money at stake as well as his two children. Divorce is the least appealing side of the law isn't it?' Dulcie said to Selina. 'When he was first training for the bar Piers worked for a firm of divorce lawyers. In many ways I blame that period for the cynicism I see in him now. You've met my son, Selina?'

'Yes, briefly.' She wouldn't have said anything more, but the Judge overheard them and laughed. 'I should say so, Dulcie, I was privileged to witness her giving that son of yours a most definite put-down.' He went on to quickly explain what had happened, making the small incident seem far more dramatic than it had actually been. 'I warned her that Piers wouldn't take too kindly to her rebuff,' he concluded smiling at Selina.

'Henry, you're embarrassing Selina,' Susan Seaton told her husband chidingly.' He was using a little of his court room licence there, Dulcie, I'm afraid,' she told her friend. 'All Selina did was refuse Piers' invitation to dance. After all he *was* with another girl at the time,' she added.

'Yes, I'm afraid my son is inclined to behave rather cavalierly when the mood takes him. A result of losing his father at a very impressionable age. Fortunately my brother stepped in before too much damage was done, but Piers had inherited more than his fair share of the Harvey pig-headedness. Gerald has at least learned to temper his a little, although it's still there, witness the battle we had to get him to employ an assistant. I shudder to think what would happen if he and Piers ever really clashed.'

As the Seaton's maid appeared at that moment to announce lunch the conversation came to a close. Selina found to her dismay that she was seated next to Harry; and moreover that he was intent on making himself as obnoxious as possible.

'How about letting me take you out to dinner tonight?' he invited when she had removed his hand from her knee for the third time. 'I know this little place…'

'Thank you, but I already have a date.' It was Selina's stock-in-trade lie, which she had found far more effective than an outright refusal.

'Have you indeed?' Interest sharpened the dark eyes. 'Well, well and I thought you were quite the little hermit. Anyone I know?' The question was asked casually, but Selina felt his tension. Ever since she had first been introduced to him two years ago Harry had been trying to persuade her to go out with him. Although she didn't have much contact with the other secretaries and staff who worked for men in the close-knit circle of which the Judge was a part, she had heard various rumours that Harry considered himself something of a Don Juan.

Unlike Piers Gresham he did not possess that aura of intense masculine sexuality which she found so frightening, and because of it he was much easier to deal with. Even so she was relieved when the end of the meal released her from his company.

'Harry proving rather over-amorous?' Dulcie Gresham asked sympathetically joining Selina over by one of the windows. 'That young man really does lack manner I'm afraid.'

'He'll soon weary of the chase,' the Judge comforted Selina. 'He lacks staying power— unlike some I could name,' he added to Dulcie with a chuckle. 'Now I couldn't see that son of yours letting anything stop him getting something he wanted.'

'Umm...' A little to Selina's surprise, her response was not totally approving. 'I'm afraid that Piers still has to learn to temper his judgments with compassion, and I think one or two set-backs might just hasten that process. Although in many ways his determination is an asset, in others it isn't. It gives him the power to overcome those who are weaker than him too easily—not always a good thing.'

The Seatons excused themselves to chat to their other guests and as though sensing Selina's surprise, Dulcie Gresham said humorously, 'Did you expect me to be a totally doting mother? Well, in many ways I am, but my love for him doesn't blind me entirely to Piers' faults. I don't know if you're aware of it or not, but my brother suffered a most appalling scandal when he was younger. Piers was eight at the time and adored my brother.' A frown touched Dulcie Gresham's expertly made up face. 'It didn't help that Piers had been involved in the scandal—whether by accident or design I do not know—in that the woman concerned had visited him at school with my brother. I was away in the States at the time. Although Piers never really talked much about it, I suspect he suffered a feeling of betrayal. My brother was his God in many ways…and I think he felt that he'd been used. However, that's all water under the bridge now, but I have the sneaky feeling that Piers transferred all the bad feelings he felt from my brother to his woman friend. Certainly he treats the majority of our sex with a cynicism I find hard not to criticise at times. No doubt he'll be one of those men who marry late in life; probably a sweet young thing who he'll always hold at a slight distance. That thought saddens me very much. I had such happiness with his father. Piers tends to dismiss my views as romantic, I know, but he is after all my son, and very much a Harvey. I just hope he doesn't discover too late that even cynics fall in love.

'You don't think I should be telling you all this do you?' she asked, surprising Selina with her perception. 'Perhaps not. Certainly Piers would be furious, but Henry was right you know. He won't take your rejection kindly— Oh I'm not suggesting he'll take it out on you professionally. He might have faults, but I don't believe small-mindedness is one of them, but he's a man who isn't used to female rejection, Selina, and if you'll take my advice you'll tread warily with him. I should hate to see you hurt.'

'But you hardly know me.' For once Selina could not disguise her feelings.

The blue eyes so like her son's softened. 'Perhaps not, but I feel as though I know you.'

In order to avoid Harry, Selina decided to leave

early. She found her hosts deep in conversation with another couple and politely interrupted to say her goodbyes.

'Selina, you must come round one night next week, and tell us all about your new job,' the Judge insisted. Promising to do so, she looked round for Dulcie Gresham, but there was no sign of the older woman. Quenching a small stab of disappointment that she had left without seeking her out, Selina went upstairs to claim her coat. She too had felt at ease with her in a way she had never expected; but then of course, she wasn't simply Piers Gresham's mother; she was also her aunt. It was like unlocking the door to a hidden pain; the old childish resentment of her father's legitimate children came gushing back; *they* had not been rejected by their father; they had not had to endure the taunts of their peers; the knowledge that their mother lived with a succession of men.

Stop it, stop it, she cautioned herself. Encouraging those sort of feelings would cause her nothing but anguish; she had taught herself that long long ago. At university she had realised that she had to disassociate herself from her burden

of guilt if she was to live in peace. The guilt was
not hers, and surely if she told herself that firmly
and often enough, she would come to believe
it.

She was so wrapped up in her thoughts that she
didn't see the other two people in the hallway
until she reached it. The colour receded quickly
from her face as she saw Piers Gresham standing
beside his mother chatting with the Seatons.

'Selina, my dear, there you are.' Dulcie
Gresham greeted her warmly. 'I was just asking
Susan where you were. I would have hated to
leave without saying goodbye. Piers, why on
earth didn't you tell me what a charming girl
Selina is?'

His mother was laying it on a trifle thickly
Selina thought, but she was still unable to repress
the small gleam of amusement that lit her eyes,
a totally natural smile curving her mouth.

'Perhaps because I suspected it was something
you'd soon discover for yourself,' Piers drawled,
helping his mother on with her coat. His voice
was mild, but there was nothing mild about the
look he gave Selina. It dulled the light in her eyes
instantly, her mouth freezing in its half-smile as

she caught the full force of his icy stare. That she should be amused by his mother's comment plainly infuriated him and he was making no bones about letting her know it.

Turning away Selina felt her heart plummet as Harry strolled into the hall. On seeing her there he exclaimed triumphantly. 'Just going… You must let me give you a lift. Now…no protests, I know you don't have a car.'

Before she could speak, Selina heard Dulcie Gresham saying calmly, 'No need for that, Harry, we're dropping Selina off. Come along, dear,' she added, touching her arm. 'Best not to keep Piers waiting, he does hate it so, but then I suppose you've noticed that already.'

Too bemused to protest, Selina let herself be shepherded towards the door, unhappily aware of the speculation and chagrin in Harry's eyes as he glanced from Piers to herself. No doubt he was assuming that Piers was the 'date' she had fibbed to him about. Well, it was scarcely important, she told herself, taking a deep breath as the front door closed behind them.

'It was very kind of you to rescue me like that,' she began, refusing to look at Piers, but all too aware of his dark, magnetic presence behind her, 'but really I can make my own way home.'

'Nonsense.' Dulcie's tone was brisk. 'Of course we will give you a lift.'

'Perhaps Miss Thorn is trying delicately to inform us that she would have preferred to accept Harry's invitation,' Piers put in smoothly. 'After all, Mother dear, you didn't actually give her any chance to respond.'

'Selina loathes the man,' his mother told him succinctly. 'And don't be so pedantic, Piers. I'm not a member of one of your juries you know. You didn't want to go with Harry, did you, Selina?'

She was caught in a trap. If she told the truth she would be obliged to accept the lift that Dulcie had offered, and yet she could hardly be more unaware of Piers' disinclination to give her a lift.

In the end she opted for the middle road. 'I didn't particularly want to go with Harry, no, but you really need not give me a lift. The tube is very convenient.'

'There you are, Mother.' Piers' voice was oddly harsh. 'Miss Thorn has as little liking for our company as she does the obnoxious Harry's. And

since she's old enough to make her own deci-
sions I suggest we allow her to do so.'

'Piers, really!'

Selina could tell both from his mother's expression and voice that she genuinely was embarrassed. Wanting to put her at her ease she said
quickly, 'No, really, Mr Gresham is quite
right…I…' She turned away and rushed down
the drive, not wanting either of them to see the
sudden sheen of tears she knew was in her eyes.
Why did she never learn, she demanded fiercely
of herself as she made her way home; why had
she laid herself so open to his contempt and humiliation. She had known from the first what
manner of man he was. Perhaps if she had not
refused to dance with him in quite such strong
terms they might…but no…he had openly
admitted that he was suspicious of her, Selina
reminded herself.

What had she let herself in for in giving in to
the compulsion to know more of her father? It
was too late to turn back and yet every instinct
she possessed warned her to keep away from
Piers Gresham; to avoid him at all costs.
Unwittingly, she touched her mouth, withdraw-

ing her fingers as though they burned when she realised what she was doing. Just for a moment she had been reliving the pressure of his mouth on hers; fierce and angry, communicating to her a thousand emotions too complex to analyse but which had somehow pierced all her barriers and distrust of his sex to provoke from her a physical response which still had the power to disturb her.

CHAPTER THREE

IT was several weeks before Selina saw Dulcie Gresham again, and then only by chance. She had slipped into a local record shop on impulse during her lunch hour, tempted inside by a window display which featured a Vivaldi recording she had coveted for a long time. Music was one of her great passions, and having just received her salary cheque there was no reason why she should not indulge herself a little.

Dulcie Gresham spotted her while she was studying the recordings on offer.

'Selina, my dear,' she exclaimed touching her lightly on the arm. 'What a piece of good luck, I have been meaning to call in at chambers for some time to see you, but somehow or other other things have intervened. Ah, you are tempted by the Vivaldi I see. They're having a brief season of his work at the Opera House soon. I'm a great Vivaldi fan myself, I don't suppose you'd consider keeping me company there one evening?'

Selina knew she ought to refuse. Dulcie Gresham was her employer's sister and the mother of a man who had been bluntly rude about his suspicions of her, and yet, half-bemused by the invitation, she heard herself accepting. She liked Dulcie Gresham; there was no getting away from it. She was a woman of her time, but she had a strength that Selina felt drawn to.

'Good girl. I normally would have gone with Piers, but he's very tied up with a new case at the moment.' She gave Selina a thoughtful look. 'I must apologise for his rude behaviour the other week.'

'There's really no need,' Selina forced a smile. 'I'm afraid the plain truth is that your son and I simply don't get on.'

'Umm…' This time the look she gave Selina made the latter colour slightly defensively. 'Yes, I'm afraid it is mutual, although in your son's case his dislike of me is intensified by the fact that he's decided my presence as Sir Gerald's PA is motivated by some dark and sinister purpose.'

It was impossible not to keep a faint bitterness out of her voice and on the point of marvelling at how easy she found it to speak freely to this woman of all women, Selina was checked by the thread of amusement in her voice when she said solemnly, 'You don't say? Good heavens, he must have a far more inventive imagination than I ever dreamed. Seriously, my dear,' she added gently, 'I suspect a good deal of this antipathy that exists between you springs from nothing more than hurt male pride, although I'm sure he'd be furious to hear me say as much. My son prides himself on his logical mind; he tends to forget that he is as equally vulnerable to human emotions as the rest of us, unfortunately.'

Selina didn't have much of her lunch hour left, and because hearing his mother talk about him to her in a way she knew he would resent made her feel acutely uncomfortable for some reason, she made her excuses and hurried back to the office.

Sir Gerald was out for lunch and she intended to make good use of his absence to catch up on her work. They had developed a good working relationship; she had discovered in him an ability to condense even the most complicated information in a way that made listening to him an education. There were times it was true when she was almost overwhelmed by the need to turn to him and tell him who she was, but she knew deep inside herself that she never would. She cherished the tenuous link of affection that was developing between them too much to hazard it by telling him the truth and seeing him withdraw from her. She had been right in thinking that applying for this post could cause her pain; and yet there was a joy mingled with that pain. She was learning to know the father she had never had as a child, and although sometimes she was contemptuous of herself for taking so much pleasure from so little she knew that if that link was severed now it would cause her to suffer.

When Sir Gerald returned Piers was with him. In her own mind now Selina had got used to calling her father 'Sir Gerald' and she responded warmly to his smile when he walked in, until she realised he wasn't alone.

'I want to go over the Hardwicke case with Piers,' he told her. 'There are several aspects of it that I'm not happy with. Could you bring us the file please, Selina. Oh, and I'd like you to stay and take a few notes.'

One of the first things Selina had done since starting her job had been to sort through the files. The wealth of legal documents and notices each one held was far too complex for Sue, the secretary, to be able to handle and now each file possessed a chart just inside the front cover, documenting its progress.

Piers frowned briefly when she placed the file on the desk between the two men. She had not seen much of him at all, much to her relief, but she could tell from the way his cool gaze rested on her for a second that he had not changed his mind about her; he still did not trust her. She moved the file closer to her father and in doing so tautened the fabric of her silk blouse across her breasts. Her movement had not been a provocative one and yet she was instantly aware of Piers' attention switching from the file to her body. Anger fired through her as she was forced to withstand his openly sexual appraisal of her, but she banked it down, not wanting to give him the satisfaction of provoking a response. It was far better to simply pretend that she was unaware of his scrutiny.

She thought she had succeeded until Sir Gerald excused himself from the office to go and give Sue a message for a client he was expecting. As soon as they were alone Piers lifted his eyes from the document he was studying and said, 'What is it about my looking at you that makes you feel so uncomfortable I wonder?'

Infuriated both by his arrogant air of superiority and her own response to it she retaliated curtly, 'That wasn't discomfort it was annoyance—exactly the same annoyance you would feel were a woman to look at you in the way you were looking at me.'

'Would I?' His mouth curved cynically, 'Who knows; perhaps if I were in your shoes I should feel flattered.'

Selina was so angry that she almost wanted to hit him. 'Well if you were you'd be remarkably foolish,' she told him crisply, 'because there is nothing complimentary about being regarded as a sexual object.'

His eyebrows rose, and Selina could have sworn there was a tinge of amusement in his eyes. 'Oh, is that what you thought I was doing?' His voice was languidly soft; and she could well imagine the effect of that cool drawl on a pent-up witness. 'I thought I was simply admiring the shape and firmness of your breasts.'

His effrontery took her breath away. How could he tell her one day that he mistrusted her, and then the next day talk about admiring her body? He could do it because he was an extremely devious man, Selina told herself. He had not forgotten their encounter in the restaurant; she was sure of that; and neither had he changed his opinion of her, so why then the deliberate attempt to over-whelm and disarm? Did he think to confuse her with signals that he found her sexually attractive, to such an extent that he could discover whatever it was he thought she was hiding. She almost laughed out loud. He had absolutely no chance.

She was almost on the point of demanding what game he thought he was playing when Sir Gerald came back. The two men soon became re-engrossed in the work on hand but Selina couldn't settle. Despite her attempts to blot it out, her mind kept showing her pictures of Piers; coolly arrogant and entirely male. What would he be like when he made love? That she should even have the thought shocked her, shocked and excited, she admitted inwardly on a small shiver, trying to imagine the saturnine features transformed by desire; the hard male body possessed by passion. It seemed incredible that after so many years of successfully blocking out any sexual desire or need from her mind and body she should find it so difficult to continue doing so now; and worse that Piers Gresham of all men should be the one to instigate such thoughts. God, if he ever found out… She closed her eyes and opened them to find Sir Gerald studying her with kind concern.

'Selina, my dear, you've gone quite pale. Are you all right?'

'Just a little tired.' It was true. She had spent the previous three evenings repainting her small kitchen, staying up later than usual to do so.

'Poor Miss Thorn,' Piers mocked. 'You really must tell your boyfriend to get you home earlier; either that or move in with him.'

'Piers, you're embarrassing the girl.' His uncle's reproof was mild.

'Oh I shouldn't think so. Sex isn't a subject that causes embarrassment to today's younger generation is it, Miss Thorn?'

Although he had asked her the question Selina suspected that he knew exactly how difficult she found it not to shrink away from it; just as she suspected he had guessed that any discussion concerning sex did embarrass her.

'Not when it's discussed objectively,' she replied as calmly as she could. 'But my private life is private, and I don't care to have it made the subject of general office discussion.' She knew that she sounded prim and spinsterish, so she added recklessly, 'I'm sure you wouldn't care to have me comment on your sex life.'

'Not unless you were speaking from first-hand experience.'

Selina froze in her chair, not daring to look either at Sir Gerald or at her tormentor. Picking up her book and pencil she said stiffly, 'I have some work to do on the Letford case, Sir Gerald, I'll be in my office if you need me.'

As she was closing the door, she heard Sir Gerald saying far less mildly to his nephew. 'That was rather under the belt, Piers. What the devil's got into you?'

She closed the door behind her without waiting to hear Piers' response. His attitude towards her today had been unforgivable, and she sensed that unless she could come to terms with it he was going to make her life while she was at work a misery. Perhaps that was the whole idea, she thought cynically; make her so unhappy that she'd leave. But she wasn't going to do that; the same stubborn determination that had helped her through her childhood and adolescence, wouldn't let her give in to his bullying any more than it had let her give in to that of her peers. Besides, the delicate relationship she was developing with her father was far too precious to relinquish.

She didn't hear from Dulcie Gresham until the week before the concert. Her 'phone was ringing one evening when she got home from work and to her surprise when she picked up the receiver Dulcie was on the other end of the line. 'I'm just ringing to confirm our arrangements for next week,' she told Selina. 'I've got the tickets; it starts at 7.00 and I thought we'd have supper together afterwards if that's all right with you. I'm really looking forward to it,' she added, 'and to seeing you.'

It was ironic that this friendship should be developing between her and the woman who was really her aunt, and there was a bond of kinship between them; Selina had felt it too. No doubt Piers would disapprove, well let him, she thought childishly. He hadn't said anything else to her, but whenever he was around she sensed him watching her, waiting for her to make a false move, no doubt.

Almost as though she had read his mind the very next day he walked into her office just before lunch. She was alone, having promised to keep an ear out for the phones for Sue, who shared the room with her, the other girl having nipped out early for lunch.

The moment she saw his face, Selina knew that his visit was not a friendly one. His expression was grimly angry, no warmth or amusement in his eyes today as they raked her slender frame from head to foot. 'All right, what's it all about?' he demanded without preamble. 'What's all this about you going out with my mother?'

Just for a moment Selina quailed beneath his icily controlled anger, but her spirit re-asserted itself and she returned his look with an equally disdainful one of her own, her chin tilting defiantly as she looked at him. 'Your mother very kindly invited me to accompany her to a Vivaldi concert and I agreed.'

'So she tells me…Vivaldi? I shouldn't have thought that was your scene…'

The arrogance of his assumptions about her was infuriating. Her fingers curled angrily into her palms and the weight of twenty-four years of rejection and taunting was behind her as she said scornfully, 'Shouldn't you? Why not I wonder? Aren't humble PAs allowed to enjoy the classics? Just because we do not aspire to the heights inhabited by superior beings such as yourself must that mean that our tastes and dreams must be as squalid as our lives sometimes have to be?' She was in a fine temper now, her cheeks flushed; her eyes a deep smokey amethyst. 'How dare you sit in judgment on me?' she demanded huskily. 'How dare you make arrogant and incorrect assumptions about me? You know nothing about me…nothing at all…'

The force with which he grasped her upper arms at any other time would have made her wince in pain, but now she was too angry to feel anything other than the rip tide of adrenalin flooding through her veins.

'I know you're not here simply because you want a job,' he told her thickly. 'Every instinct I possess tells me that… Why are you cultivating my mother? What do you hope to gain from her? An introduction to a wealthy mate?'

His cynicism stunned her. How dared he assume that she wanted anything? How dared he catalogue her as a scheming, grasping woman bent on using everyone who came her way, for her own selfish ends…?

'Don't think I haven't seen the way you pander to my uncle,' he told her raspingly, before she could speak, 'but you're wasting your time there, it's been tried before…'

For a moment she was terrorised by the fear that he would suddenly realise who she was, but almost immediately it receded to be replaced by a tearingly bitter pain. Unable to cope with the implications of it she lashed out bitterly, 'And of course your concern is only for your uncle; your motives completely pure and having nothing to do with…'

'With what?' he asked her gratingly. 'The fact that sexually I find you desirable? Not to the extent that my need to possess you outweighs everything else. You have the intelligence to be doing a job far more demanding than this; you could use it to forge a career for yourself, but you haven't done, have you? No. Why I wonder?'

'Then keep on wondering.' Selina snapped bitingly back at him. 'Because you'll never find out from me!'

'You think not. I wouldn't bank on it, my dear.' He was sneering at her now and Selina found it incredible that he could ever have admitted wanting her. 'There are ways of making even the stubbornest person talk.'

'Is that how you win your cases?' Her own voice was as cutting as his now. 'By bludgeoning your victims verbally until you're ready to confess to anything to escape you?'

'I think you're accrediting me with powers no human being could possibly possess.' He drawled the words in cool mockery, but there was a tinge of dark colour burning along his cheek-bones that told Selina that her jibe had gone home.

'I take it you still intend to attend the concert with my mother?'

'Unless she changes her mind.'

'I don't want you involved with my family,

Miss Thorn,' he told her cruelly. 'In fact I find the very idea extremely disturbing.'

'All because you suspect me of some unknown ulterior motive?' She was using words to conceal from him her pain. 'What is it you're frightened I might do? Steal the silver?'

'Don't push me too far,' he warned her quietly. 'Believe me right at this minute, it wouldn't take very much to push me over the edge.'

Selina could well believe it, but she wasn't going to be browbeaten into giving up her friendship with his mother she told herself stubbornly, ten minutes later, running cold water over her wrists in the hope that somehow this would reduce her thudding pulses and cool down the hectic colour burning her skin. Now that she was safely away from him she could let her body relax and give in to the tremors of reaction shuddering through it. He found her sexually desirable he had said, but there had been no warmth in his eyes as he made the admission; no caring…nothing other than dislike and distrust.

As she prepared for her evening out with his mother, Selina forced herself to think about the implications contained within her physical responsiveness to Piers. He had breached all barriers she had put up against his sex like a ho. knife melting butter; anger; resentment; desire; none of them were emotions she had ever allowed herself to feel, or wanted to feel before. Almost without being aware of making a conscious decision on it she had grown from childhood suspicious and wary of committing herself to another human being—she had no close friends; no confidantes; no lovers past or present and yet this was the first time that she had seen that lack as something to be regretted. If she had allowed herself such relationships she might not be so acutely vulnerable to Piers now she acknowledged; she would have learned from them and been able to gauge and assess her reactions to him more realistically.

It didn't help that she also had to take into account their blood tie; they were cousins, son and daughter of a couple who were sister and brother; and yet it was laughable to imagine Piers ever accepting her as such she thought, with wry self-mockery; he would move heaven and hell to deny such a relationship; she knew that instinctively. And there could certainly be no question of her confronting him with the truth; scorning him to deny her fathering. She shivered a little, recalling his insistence that she was hiding something; that she had an ulterior purpose in working for Sir Gerald. What did he really suspect her of?

Even if she were to overcome his dislike and suspicion of her there could be no peaceful co-existence for them; not when he had admitted his sexual desire for her. She shivered a little in the warmth of her bedroom; the resentment and revulsion she ought to feel at such an admission was frighteningly lacking; rather there was a frisson of something along her spine and nerve endings that might be a reckless kind of excitement.

Every logical instinct she possessed warned her that if she did want to experiment with sex, Piers was the very last person she should choose as her partner; he would destroy her, she acknowledged inwardly, and having done so would turn his back on her without a second thought. If he didn't dislike her for any particular reason, simply the fact that he desired her would have been enough. She had sensed that when he told her about it; and male-like she would be the one he would punish for that desire; not himself.

Stop thinking about him, she told herself as she finished dressing. She hadn't been quite sure what to wear in view of the fact that they were eating out after the concert and in the end had opted for a plain silk dress in a soft grey printed with lemon and white flowers. The slightly thirties style of the dress suited her slender figure and with it she wore a plain grey jacket. Tonight for some reason she had felt impelled to do more to her appearance than usual. She had been shopping with Sue the previous lunchtime and the other girl had persuaded her to buy some new makeup. The salesgirl they had approached had been very helpful and the misty grey eye-shadow did add depth and a faint mystery to her eyes she acknowledged, studying her reflection thoughtfully.

Working for her father was changing her; she was losing her fear of other human beings and of expressing herself freely to them; she was no longer as afraid of rejection as she had once been; and yet it was not just that, she mused, looking at herself. Somehow she looked differ-ent...more alive... Shaking her head, she picked up her bag and headed into her small sitting

room. Her taxi would soon arrive. She had decorated the room herself, using primarily neutral
colours and she frowned over it now feeling that
something was missing…lacking… That was it,
she decided in surprise, it lacked colour and
warmth. Did she too project the same cold image
as her home?

Before she could dwell too long on the thought
her taxi arrived. She had arranged to meet Dulcie
Gresham just outside the Opera House, and she
eyed the crowd already gathered there with some
misgivings hoping that they would not miss one
another. Her fears were misplaced. No sooner
had she stepped out on to the pavement than
Dulcie hailed her.

Turning to greet her, Selina felt the smile
freeze on her face as she saw Piers standing
behind his mother. Her heart seemed to miss a
beat and thud erratically. Anger flashed bitterly
in her eyes for a moment as they challenged his.
What possible harm did he really think she
could do to his mother; or more to the point
want to do? If he knew the truth… It was several
seconds before she was able to acknowledge
that being the cynical soul that he was if he

knew the truth he would be at even greater pains to keep them apart.

'Isn't it marvellous,' Dulcie crowed, 'Piers was able to come after all.'

Selina felt acutely uncomfortable. 'You should have told me. Piers could have had my ticket, after all you only invited me in the first place because he could not go.'

'Rubbish.' Dulcie's voice was firm. 'I invited you because I enjoy your company. That's not to say that I'm not glad he is with us.' She turned to her son and said anxiously, 'Where's Verity, there's such a crowd here that…'

'She's here now.'

Selina's stomach muscles tightened as she saw the tall dark woman coming towards them, although older than she would have expected one of Piers' dates to be, in every other way she fulfilled her mental image of the type of woman he would escort. Dark and soignee; she wore her silk evening suit with an elegance that came from years of wearing expensive clothes. The pearls round her throat and in her ears were real, Selina suspected, and her beautifully made-up face was smooth as a girl of twenty's.

Just for a second her eyes met Piers' and as though he knew of the feelings tormenting her, his mouth twisted in a taunting smile.

'Selina come and meet my niece Verity Graham.'

It was so totally unexpected that Selina couldn't move. Her niece... Her eyes widened fractionally, faint colour creeping up under her skin. Unaware how closely Piers was watching her, she fought for composure.

'I believe you work for my father, Selina.' Verity's voice and smile were warm, totally without guile or suspicion. 'We've all heard what a paragon you are.'

'Oh, very much so.'

Was she the only one to hear the faint malice in Piers' drawled words. 'But I think we'd better go in. We don't want to miss anything do we?'

In other circumstances Selina would have been in seventh heaven, content simply to enjoy the music, but tonight she was unable to do so, unable to relax and stop herself from stealing glances at Verity Graham. They were half-sisters, Selina thought, on an inward shiver...suddenly overwhelmed by a surge of emotion so strong that she felt tears prick her eyes. Fortunately the others were too engrossed in the music to notice her emotionalism, or at least she thought they were until she saw Piers looking frowningly at the betraying handkerchief balled up in her small fist. Let him stare, she thought stubbornly; let him think what he liked; only she knew the truth.

Being brought face-to-face with one of her half-sisters so unexpectedly robbed her of any desire to eat. She had already decided before they left the concert hall that she would bow out of the supper and go straight home, but as soon as she started to say so, both Dulcie and Verity started to protest.

'No please do come… I've been telling Verity about you. Like us she's another Vivaldi fan.'

'Yes,' Verity laughed. 'In fact it's something of a family joke. You see my father adores him, and so does Aunt Dulcie, but I'm the only one of his children who shares his passion for music. Mummy always says the other two take after her. In fact if James, my husband, hadn't been away on business this week I would have had to miss this concert.' She wrinkled her nose pertly.

All through her supper Selina was conscious of Piers studying her. He had been very quiet since they entered the restaurant, leaving the conversation to his mother and cousin. Selina too found she had very little to say, and when at last she left the family trio to climb into the taxi Piers had hailed for her, she let her eyes sting with fresh tears; suffering a pain she had not known since her schooldays, when the sight of happy family units had had the power to tear her apart.

Leave; an inner voice urged her as she let herself into her flat. Leave now, before it's too late, and yet she knew that, against all logic, she would not do so. Fool, fool, she chided herself and that night in bed for the first time in years she allowed herself to cry; deep, rending sobs that shook her body and soaked her pillow, leaving her feeling oddly cleansed and relaxed.

CHAPTER FOUR

AFTERWARDS she was to acknowledge that the traumatic meeting with her half-sister had marked the point where her attitudes to life began to change. It was as though seeing and talking to her had operated some secret lock allowing emotions she had denied to herself for years to become part of her life.

Almost before she had been aware of what she was doing she had trained herself to accept that her father could not exist for her and although she had daydreamed of growing up to impress and astonish him, until Judge Seaton had suggested she apply for her present job she had always shrunk from the thought of seeing him; dreading a rejection, unable to bear seeing him turn away from her in denial.

Where before she had grimly refused to allow herself to think about him or his family she had now developed an appetite to know everything about them. Occasionally after a weekend he would mention various visits from his daughters and their families. Emily, the eldest, had three children; two boys and a girl. Both boys were still at school, but the daughter, Camilla, at sixteen was apparently something of a problem. 'The only person who seems to get any response from her is Piers,' Sir Gerald confided one Monday morning. He was looking particularly worn and a sharp pang of concern for him shot through her. Oh, how creepingly dangerous was this affection for him she had scarcely expected to feel and yet which at times threatened to overcome common sense and caution; demanding the right to be voiced.

'It is very difficult for her, of course,' he added with grandfatherly indulgence. 'She is nowhere near as clever as her brothers, but still bright enough to be aware of it, I'm afraid. Emily and her husband are divorced.' He grimaced faintly. 'They parted when Camilla was at a very vulnerable age. The more I see of the effects of divorce the less sure I am about its efficacy. Perhaps our ancestors had the right idea after all when they married for less romantic reasons. Love, which in these supposedly enlightened times, is often nothing more than acute sexual lust is not any lasting basis for a relationship. I expect you find me very cynical,' he continued wryly, 'but I'm afraid the older one gets and the more one observes of life the more convinced I am that the human race possesses an instinct for self-destruction that is truly appalling.'

He caught her expression and smiled faintly. 'Am I depressing you, Selina? I forget sometimes how young you are; just a few years older than Camilla, and yet you have a maturity that often makes me think we're of the same generation. The family unit is still a very strong institution... Dulcie and I are closer now perhaps than we ever were as children.'

'I've always wished I wasn't an only one.' The admission was out before she could silence it; the echo of a passionate childhood desire to have someone to share the trauma of those years with.

'You have no family at all?' His voice was compassionate and Selina wished passionately that they had never entered these dangerous conversational waters. 'None,' she told him crisply, and then more as a warning to herself than anything else, she added. 'Somewhere I have a father, but doubt that he ever gives any thought to me.' Bitter pain darkened her eyes as she spoke, unaware that Piers had walked into the room and overheard her last words.

When she did see him, humiliation that she should have witnessed a betrayal of her feelings sent colour to her pale skin, her desire to escape his presence so great that she was unaware of his frowning concentration on her comment.

Work kept her mind occupied during the day. Occasionally she spoke to Dulcie Gresham when she telephoned to speak to her brother, but there had been no repeat invitations. No doubt Piers had advised his mother against involving herself socially with the help, she thought bitterly.

One Monday morning Sir Gerald arrived in chambers looking particularly fatigued. They had had the whole family over for the weekend, he explained to Selina, as it had been his wife's birthday. 'Grandchildren are delightful, but exhausting,' he told Selina wryly, as he settled down to work, 'but Mary adores them and loves nothing more than a family "do".'

Maybe so, but couldn't she see how tired and strained her husband was looking, Selina wondered, and then berated herself for the thought and for the emotional involvement behind it. What was she doing working here, allowing herself to be drawn into a relationship which could only ever be one-sided? Did she always want to sit on the sidelines of life, watching while others participated?

Piers came in with a bulky folder under his arm while they were talking. 'The Hargreaves case comes up next week,' he told his uncle abruptly. 'There's a couple of points I'm concerned about.'

The case in question was the divorce he was handling for a friend of his mother's—a woman whose husband was deserting her for a girl twenty years younger, and Selina shivered uncontrollably as she was forced to sit and listen to the two men discussing the case, the relationship between the three main parties too close to that which had existed between Sir Gerald and her own mother for her to listen with equanimity.

'Sophie Hargreaves is distraught,' Selina heard Piers telling Sir Gerald. 'The girl in question is the daughter of a friend—her own father has recently been declared bankrupt and no doubt she sees Alan as a handy substitute. He, poor fool, is too besotted to realise the truth.'

Sir Gerald's mild, 'The girl might genuinely care for him, Piers,' was greeted with a harsh disclaimer. 'I doubt it very much. Take away his bank balance and you take away the prime cause of her "love". In five years time, if she's still with him, he'll be bitterly regretting it. He'd have been far better keeping his marriage intact and paying for his pleasure on the side—he'd have got a damn sight better value for money that way.'

'Piers, you're a cynic,' Sir Gerald told him. He looked at Selina and smiled wryly, 'Selina, my dear, I'm afraid my sex is always very vulnerable in its vanity and thirst for feminine flattery. And the older we get, I'm afraid the more vulnerable we become.'

She suspected that it was an oblique reference to his own involvement with her mother, and her heart started to pound. She felt sick and giddy and was overcome by an urgent desire to escape from the office. She couldn't sit there under Piers' sharp critical eye and not betray what she was feeling. She had never had any illusions about her mother, but in the last few years she had come to accept her weaknesses without taking the guilt of them on her own shoulders, and now in the space of a mere half an hour all that guilt was back; she felt almost as though she *were* her mother; the type of woman whom Piers so clearly despised; the woman who had tried to use their sexual relationship to force from her father the security of marriage and the ability to enjoy his wealth.

The papers had been cruel in their denouncement of her, and she had read every single one. What she had read had left her scarred and hurt and she shuddered now, wondering what Piers' reaction would be if she stood up and announced her identity. Some wilful part of her almost wanted her to do it; to shout it as loud as she could; to throw off the burden of guilt and say this is what I am, and I'm not ashamed of it.

But she was; deep down inside she was ashamed. She smiled grimly to herself... The sins of the fathers...or in this case of the mother... The man who wrote that truly knew what he was saying.

As the summer recess drew nearer the pace of work hotted up. Sir Gerald was often absent from the office at court. Occasionally Selina went with him and found these occasions fascinating and exciting, although occasionally she wondered if she would have had the detachment necessary to make a first-rate barrister.

Sir Gerald often discussed the technique of his colleagues with her, and one day as they were setting out for court he took her by surprise by saying, 'Piers is in court today. If our case finishes early, as I think it might, we might go and listen to his. He's a first rate counsel and he's lucky in that he possesses a rare additional gift; he has an intuition about people that's almost faultless. I say almost because Piers is as vulnerable to the old prejudice as the rest of the human race.'

Selina had a first-hand opportunity to see just what Sir Gerald meant later that day. As he had predicted his own case closed just before lunch and after the recess he directed her to the court where Piers' was sitting.

It was the first time she had seen him dressed in his court robes and the sight of him sitting in consultation with his colleagues brought a tension to the pit of her stomach that was instantly betraying.

Pity the poor defendant who had to face him, she thought shivering slightly. In his black robes, he looked like some dark avenging Lucifer. Telling herself she was being ridiculously fanciful, she tried to concentrate on the case. It was a rape case and a particularly unpleasant one at that. The girl, an eighteen-year-old, was pregnant and was claiming that she had been raped by a friend of the family who had called round when her parents were absent.

The man in question, dressed formally in a business suit, well-groomed but pale, was Piers' client. He spoke in a low voice and displayed a surprising firmness when it came to resisting the verbal thrusts of the prosecution.

The girl, on the other hand, looked frail and heart-rendingly defenceless. Her swollen stomach was almost grotesque against the acute thinness of the rest of her body. She broke down twice during the questioning of her own counsel, and Selina felt her muscles clench in protest when Piers approached her and began his cross examination.

It was a nightmare that seemed to go on without end, punctuated by the sobs of the girl in the witness box. At one point Selina thought she would be unable to endure any more. She longed to stand up and demand that the torment was stopped. How could these others sit here and listen impassively to what Piers was doing? He questioned her ruthlessly, naming several youths who had claimed to be her lovers. Her innocence, her character, were ruthlessly torn to shreds and in the end Selina was not all surprised when the jury found for the defence.

Afterwards, when Piers joined them, she could hardly contain her feelings. While Sir Gerald was congratulating him on his win she looked the other way.

'Something wrong, Selina?'

How smooth and self-assured his tone, like a cat fed on cream, and it sickened her to know that the cream was the total humiliation of a member of her own sex.

'Forgive me if I don't add my congratulations,' she said brittlely too wrought up to remember that she was a mere employee. 'How could you do that?' she added fiercely when he simply looked at her, watching her. 'How could you destroy that girl like that?'

'What I said was simply the truth…'

'That because she had had other lovers she could not possibly be raped?' The bitterness inside her spilled over into her voice.

She saw his lips tighten. 'I'm not such a chauvinist, Miss Thorn, no matter what you might think. In this case I assure you the man was innocent.'

'How do you know?' she demanded scornfully. 'What makes you so sure you are right? Your instincts?'

She caught the way he exhaled through gritted teeth as she flung the last comment at him and she knew he hadn't forgotten, any more than she had, his accusations to her.

'Yes…plus the fact that not ten minutes ago in the Judge's chamber she broke down and admitted to her parents that the child was a fellow schoolmate's. Her parents didn't even realise she was having sex with anyone, and too frightened to admit the truth she made up a cock-and-bull story about my client, when she realised she was not going to be able to hide her pregnancy for much longer.'

Selina was dumb-founded. She had been completely taken in by the girl's story and it galled her to know that she had been deceived. 'Which of us is guilty of chauvinism now?' Piers asked quietly, before turning on his heel and striding away.

'I'm sorry about that,' she apologised to Sir Gerald.

'No need to be,' he assured her easily. 'Rape cases are notoriously hard to handle. In this case Piers played a hunch and was proved right… that's what I meant about him being a first-rate barrister.'

'And if he had been defending the girl,' Selina asked slowly, 'would he then have attempted to conceal the truth?'

'No, knowing Piers. I suspect he would have gone for a settlement in Judge's chambers— always supposing he had allowed the case to get that far. A barrister is always at liberty to refuse a brief, and I've known Piers refuse a fair few. I know you and he don't always hit it off,' he told her with a smile, 'but under that harsh exterior, he can be surprisingly emotional.' He gave her a brief look and smiled, 'Don't judge him too harshly. Life hasn't been entirely easy for him. He was very close to his father and his death hit him hard, and then…' He broke off to return the greeting of an acquaintance and the conversation was never resumed. What had he been going to say, Selina wondered that night as she prepared for bed.

Piers was thirty-three years old and as far as she knew had no permanent relationship in his life. His mother had spoken of her wish to see him married and he was so devastatingly sexually attractive that she could not imagine his single state was anything other than voluntary, but why? He was a complex invulnerable man who, for reasons of his own, had set up many barriers against her sex, and who had also instigated himself as her enemy, she reminded herself. He didn't like her and he didn't trust her. But he *did* desire her; and she knew now with a sudden flash of intuition that he had told her so in order that he could transfer the burden of controlling that desire from himself to her and that to allow him to express it physically to her now was to accept his parameters for such a relationship. That meant she knew that it would be totally devoid of emotion or commitment; that it would simply be a satisfaction of physical lust.

A long shudder passed through her body as she forced herself to admit how vulnerable she was to him. There were times when she hated him so acutely that she longed to lash out and hurt him, but that hatred was simply the reverse side of a coin whose other side was love. But how could she love him? She tried to examine her emotions logically. What did she know of him after all, other than what she saw; what was there about him that drew her to him? He was physically attractive yes—indeed to describe him as attractive was a gross understatement—devastatingly male would be a closer description, and yet it was not simply his looks. Then what? His personality? Was she really so masochistic that she could only respond emotionally to the type of man who was bound to hurt her? There was no future in loving him, she knew that. She got up and moved restlessly round her small sitting room.

Even if by some remote possibility he should come to desire her to the extent that he was prepared to forego his suspicions of her, how could she tell him the truth? The moment he learned her identity, he would reject her, she was convinced of it. She shivered, and clutched her arms around her in a defensive motion. If she was wise she would simply smother what she felt for him; destroy it in its early stages before it took too powerful a hold on her. She had always sworn she would not make herself vulnerable through love and yet here she was abandoning everything she had ever taught herself, and for a man who could never want or love her in return.

As the summer recess drew nearer Selina could feel her tension increasing, and not purely because of her feelings for Piers. During the summer Sir Gerald worked from home. When she had accepted the job she had known this and discounted it as a problem. Now she was not so sure. She had met one of his daughters and had liked her, but how would she cope with meeting his wife; with continuing her deception in the face of his legal family?

Slowly she had come to terms with the reality of working for her father, but how would she feel when she saw him against the background of his family, giving to his other children the love he had never given her? Would she be jealous? Bitter? Coming to know him as an adult she had been surprised by her own lack of resentment towards him; he had a quick mind and a compassion for his fellow beings that warmed her; they shared a sense of humour and he often evinced a moral code so much in accordance with her own that she suspected he, too, had not come unscathed through his relationship with her mother. At times the urge to talk to him about the past to find out if indeed he ever thought about her, was almost unbearable, but she always managed to contain herself, reminding herself of Pandora's box and the havoc that opening it created.

'I shan't be sorry when recess starts,' he told her one Wednesday afternoon. 'I'm beginning to think Mary is right when she tells me I'm not as young as I was.'

Selina had noticed the lines of strain round his eyes and it worried her that he should admit to being tired; normally he resisted every suggestion that he might be overworking. She also noticed that he was massaging his left arm, and hideous thoughts of heart attacks flooded her brain.

'You've got a free afternoon today,' she

reminded him, 'why don't you take a few hours off?'

'Umm…that might not be a bad idea. I could take the papers for the Easton case with me and study them. In fact I think I'll do that. I'll be able to concentrate better away from the office.'

During the week he lived in a service flat in St John's Wood, and normally his wife lived with him, Selina knew, but the previous weekend she had elected to stay down in Dorset to get the house ready for a summer influx of grandchildren.

When he had gone she settled down to her own work, trying not to think about Piers, who had been away for several days. He was due back tomorrow and as always at the thought of seeing him, her stomach muscles tensed.

It was just gone five-thirty and she was about to leave when her phone rang. She picked it up, slightly surprised to hear Sir Gerald's voice. 'Selina, my dear, I've just discovered that I didn't bring some of the papers home with me, and I rather need to discuss them with Piers. I'm seeing him tonight, he's calling round here later, could I ask you to bring them round for me— there's no immediate rush. Go home and have something to eat first, if you prefer, Piers isn't due until around ten.'

After giving her instructions on where to find what he wanted Sir Gerald rang off. Selina found the papers without any undue difficulty and putting them in an envelope, finished clearing her desk.

Because they were busy she had worked through her lunch hour and the thought of waiting to eat until after she had been to St John's Wood was unappealing, so she decided she would eat first and then take a taxi to Sir Gerald's.

Although it was only May they had been having a brief spell of hot weather and her small flat felt stuffy and overwarm. The hunger that had been gnawing at her since mid-afternoon vanished in the clammy heat, but she forced herself to prepare a small salad and after she had eaten it, went into her bathroom to have a shower. She was very particular about eating well-balanced meals. Living alone was a constant temptation to snack, and although she had no weight problem, she was very conscious of the importance of a good diet. Her shower helped to revive her, leaving her feeling cooler and more relaxed. It was silly to feel so wrought up simply because she was visiting her father's home, she told herself, but the nervous butterflies would not go away.

Her hair had a natural wave and because she always had it well cut, was relatively easy to style. For the office she often wore it up, but tonight to save time she left it down on her shoulders, adding a frosting of eye-shadow and a slick of soft rose lipstick before leaving her mirror. Her office clothes consisted of neat suits and blouses but tonight on some impulse she pulled on jeans and a T-shirt, grimacing faintly at her own reflection before leaving her bedroom. She had lost weight and the jeans clung to her hip bones, giving her an air of fragility. Her taxi arrived on time and getting into it she subsided on the seat, giving the driver the address.

Sir Gerald's London apartment was one of five in a well-maintained Victorian house, set in impressive grounds. A little to her surprise no security system appeared to be in operation, and after checking the discreetly lettered boards in the elegant reception area she made her way to the lift. Sir Gerald's apartment was on the first floor, and on impulse instead of using the lift,

Selina chose instead to take the impressive carved wooden staircase. The wooden bannister felt smooth and warm beneath her finger-tips and she relished the sensory enjoyment of it beneath her fingers. She had always been acutely attuned to her surroundings; perhaps that was why her childhood had been so unhappy. A less sensitive child might not have reacted so badly in the same circumstances.

She reached the top of the first flight of stairs and glanced appreciatively around the small square landing. On the ceiling the Victorian plasterwork was still in place, the vine leaves delicately picked out in soft green and gold to match the pastel rug on the floor. Not Aubusson, she suspected, giving in to the impulse to bend and touch the silky fibres, but very beautiful none the less.

Straightening up, she rang the doorbell and waited. The door opened almost immediately and she stepped inside, smiling in anticipation of seeing her father. As the door swung closed behind her the smile was banished from her face, the shock of seeing Piers Gresham where she had expected her father too great for her to conceal.

That he was equally shocked was immediately evident—shocked and angry, she noted, her eyes automatically registering the fact that he had discarded his jacket, his shirt open at the throat, his hair slightly ruffled as though he had run irate fingers through it. He was tense as well, his body moving with all the lethal menace of a crouched panther.

'Sir Gerald is expecting me.' She hovered uncertainly in the foyer while Piers flung open an inner door.

'Is he now?' His voice was harsh, bitter almost. 'Come in here,' he commanded her. 'What I have to say to you isn't for general consumption.'

Numbly Selina followed him, too enmeshed in the aura of bitter violence emanating from him to argue, and found herself in an elegantly furnished drawing room, which apart from themselves was completely empty. She swung round, puzzled and apprehensive, disturbed to find he was right behind her. Her movement had brought her so close to him that she could see the tiny lines radiating outwards from his eyes; the harsh grooves of strain drawn from nose to mouth, his eyes boring into her as he registered her unease.

'My...Sir Gerald...where is he?' she asked huskily at last.

There was a tense, unnerving silence, the dark blue eyes glittered angrily over her pale face.

'My uncle, Miss Thorn,' Piers said curtly at last, 'is in hospital.'

CHAPTER FIVE

'In hospital?' Selina stared at him, too shocked to even think of concealing her emotions.

His eyes were hard as they flicked over her white face. 'Your concern for my uncle is extremely touching,' he rasped, 'but you'll have to forgive *me* if I find it somewhat suspicious. Look at you,' he commanded her, grasping her wrist and half-pulling her into the hallway, so that she faced her own reflection in a mirror hanging on the wall. The pale-faced, huge-eyed girl who stared back at her was someone she barely recognised. A wave of dizziness swept through her, and she was dimly aware that her surfeit of emotion must seem suspicious to the man holding her, but how could she explain that the emotional starvation of years had finally caught up with her, and what she was experiencing now was the fear that having met her father she was to lose him.

'Well?'

The harsh question cut painfully into her own thoughts. She turned her head and stared blindly at her interrogator, barely registering the curt demand.

'Nothing to say, is that it?'

She flinched away from his muttered curse, her body reacting like that of a stuffed sawdust doll as he shook her briefly. 'Do you realise that if you'd arrived half-an-hour ago my aunt would have been here? How do you suppose you would have felt if she'd witnessed the betraying reaction I've just seen? Are you having an affair with my uncle?'

Her dizziness cleared long enough for her to stare incredulously at him. Was *that* what he thought? She knew he had been suspicious of her motives in applying for her job, but that he should suspect this?

'Are you?'

He shook her again, and suddenly fear and pain gave way to anger. How could he be so blind? Was that really how he saw her? As a woman who would enter an affair with a man old enough to be her father and a married man at that? Hysteria bubbled wildly inside her, threatening to overset her fragile self-control.

'Well?'

'Why don't you ask Sir Gerald that himself?'

She hadn't meant to make the challenge, but somehow the words were forced out through stiff lips, the cold anger in his eyes changing to deep bitterness and then something else as he continued to hold her.

As she tried to sustain his concentrated study, fighting against the control his mind was trying to force on hers, she felt another wave of dizziness sweep back. The hallway started to sway and she felt the sharp bite of his fingers; heard the harsh expletive he uttered as she gave way to swimming darkness.

WHEN she came round she was lying on a long, cotton-covered settee with Piers standing over her, a frown of fierce concentration creasing his forehead.

'Here, drink this,' he commanded her brusquely, handing her a glass half-filled with amber liquid. She swallowed some automatically, grimacing, and then shuddering as the raw spirit hit her stomach, instinctively swinging her legs back on to the floor and struggling to sit up.

'Stay where you are,' Piers commanded curtly, 'Give yourself a chance to recover.'

'I'm surprised you didn't just throw me into the lobby,' Selina said bitterly. 'Aren't you afraid my unsavoury presence might contaminate the atmosphere?'

She watched the shrug of powerful shoulders beneath the fine silk of his shirt and was shocked by her sudden need to reach out and touch him. She wanted to feel the heat of his skin beneath her fingertips; to feel his body burn and take fire from her own, his hands and lips caressing her…

'Why did you come here?'

His abrupt question brought her back to reality.

Her chin tilted firmly as she returned his cool scrutiny. 'Sir Gerald telephoned me at the office and asked me to bring round some papers he needed. He told me there was no urgency as long as he had them some time this evening and suggested that I went home first and had my meal and then brought them. We had not arranged a clandestine lovers' meeting if that's where your fertile imagination was leading you.'

She had the satisfaction of seeing a thin, dark seeping of colour line his cheek-bones, his eyes glittering savagely as he looked down at her.

'I should have thought my uncle had more sense than to involve himself with someone like you. He's been through the traumas of an illicit affair once and it damn near destroyed both him and his family. Not that I can't see why he's tempted,' he added in a different voice, before Selina could protest her innocence. She was bitterly regretting giving in to the childish impulse she had had earlier not to answer his question directly but to refer him to Sir Gerald. Why had she done it? On some crazy hope that it might make him jealous? Now it was *her* imagination that was running away with *her*. Strangely enough she found nothing flattering in his assertion that he could see why his uncle was tempted by her. For one thing it smacked too much of the suggestion that she had been the one to involve Sir Gerald in their supposed affair instead of the other way round.

'Really?' She managed to make her voice sounded arctically indifferent, 'But unlike Sir Gerald *you* are able to resist the temptation, is that it?'

She hadn't realised how provocative her taunt was until she saw the dark colour running up under his skin and caught the savage imprecation that left his lips before his dark head bent towards her and she was imprisoned against the settee by the powerful force of his hands against her shoulders, his mouth hot and angry as it covered hers.

She knew she should be cool and withdrawn, but her need was too strong for her, and against all common sense her lips softened and clung, her arms sliding round Piers' neck to find the thick dark hair growing close to his nape. The hoarse murmur of satisfaction he made did nothing to encourage her resistance, her body as pliant and fluid as silk as he moulded it to his own, the bruising grip on her shoulders easing as his hands stroked over her back, spanning her narrow waist before reaching her hips.

It was only when she felt the hard arousal of Piers' body moving against her own that sanity intruded. She wasn't accustomed to such intimate contact with a man's body and her own reacted acutely to it, with a mingling of wanting and fear that jerked her back to reality.

She started to struggle, but Piers had manoeuvred them both so that they were lying side by side on the settee, and with her back pressed against the cushions and her front covered by the superior weight of Piers, there was no way she could win any show of physical strength.

'Stop fighting me.' His voice was thick and slightly slurred and for the first time Selina remembered that he had only arrived from the States earlier that evening, and must surely be close to the point of exhaustion. If he was, he wasn't showing it, but it could explain his behaviour. Lack of sleep could play strange tricks on one's self-control, and wanting wasn't loving, she reminded herself as she tensed her body in rejection of the male heat of his, for what had started out in anger, as a demonstration of contempt was swiftly changing course, threatening to overwhelm them both, Selina recognised as she felt Piers shudder against her, his hand cupping her breast and searing her with his heat.

'I want you.' He muttered it against her ear, his voice thick and unrecognisable, his touch sending frissons of hectic pleasure racing over her skin as his lips caressed the delicate flesh behind her ear.

Her T-shirt had become partially untucked in her struggle and when his hand slipped inside and found the rounded warmth of her breast she shivered in tense reaction, recognising that Piers' desire was fast approaching the point where it would be outside his control. If that happened and he made love to her how would he react afterwards? He would hate himself and her, Selina thought bitterly. He would hate himself for letting his guard down to such an extent that he had given in to his need to possess her and he would hate her for being a witness to what she knew he would consider to be a weakness. She had to stop him. Frantically she tried to pull away, but his free hand simply grasped the front of her shirt, wrenching it away from the waistband of her jeans as he refused to let her move.

'No!' He said the word softly, but the feverish glitter in his eyes underlined his determination. She had never seen him looking like this before, Selina thought achingly, his hair ruffled and tousled, his skin drawn tight against his cheekbones, and flushed with colour.

Like hers, his shirt had come free of his trousers, and with half of the buttons undone she could see the dark shadowing of hair against his skin. Her need to reach out and touch him shook her, overwhelming her with its intensity. Until now she had not realised how sexual hunger could be a force so strong that no mere effort of human will could overset it, but now she did and the knowledge both thrilled and frightened her. Beneath Piers' roughly caressing hand she felt her breast swell, her nipples tightening; aching. The initial savage assault of Piers' mouth on her own had changed to a series of seductively explorative kisses feathered against the skin of her face and throat; at first relaxing and now tormenting as her body yearned for a return of that earlier intense hunger.

Against all the dictates of common sense Selina found herself reaching out to touch him, prompted to do so by the deep sense of urgency he was building inside her. His thumb stroked the taut peak of her nipple and she gasped involuntarily, arching against him, feverish with need, her hand sliding inside the fine silk of his shirt to find the solid muscles of his chest. When his hand left her breast and he muttered something under his breath, her first feeling was one of sharp disappointment, followed by relief as common sense returned, only to flee again as he tore impatiently at the buttons of both their shirts, flinging his own off to reveal a torso tanned by the sun and silkily smooth apart from its shadowing of fine dark hairs. When he removed her own Selina tried to protest, panic clawing at her stomach as he unfastened her bra, but fear, panic, common sense; all of them fled as he pulled the lacy garment away and looked down at her body.

The pressure of his hand against her back had caused her to arch slightly upwards and against her will her eyes were drawn to follow the path of his as it burned over her skin, compelled by the twin crests of her breasts glowing deep pink against the delicate pallor of her skin.

This was madness, she told herself achingly… it had to stop. She lifted her arms to push him away, but all her hands encountered was the thick darkness of his hair, her closed eyes jerking open as she felt the heat of his breath searing her breasts. The touch of his mouth in the valley between them seemed to burn her skin, her urgent plea to be set free lost beneath his fierce exclamation of pleasure as his hands cupped their pale fullness and his lips burned a tortuous path towards first one summit and then the other, just stopping short of each peak and then tormenting her with lightly delicate kisses that burned rings of fire around her aching flesh.

The small sound she strangled in her throat as her fingers twined feverishly in his hair seemed to reach him despite her desire for it not to do so and his hands slid from her breasts to her waist and then down to her hips, pulling her into the aroused heat of his and holding her there, his mouth plundering hers, forcing her lips back against her teeth, inflicting an almost unbearable pleasure-pain on her senses that made her move feverishly against him, tormented by the delicate rasp of his body hair against her tender breasts; and urged on almost against her will to a fulfilment she sensed lay somewhere waiting for her.

She had enough sanity left to realise her own danger and tore her mouth from his, demanding her release in a voice that shook with all that she dared not say to him.

His response was to slide his hands slowly up her body, stopping when he reached her breasts. Without saying a word he caressed their aching fullness watching the expressions of anguish and pleasure dawn in her eyes. She must have moved, despite her determination not to do so, because suddenly she saw the flare of an answering hunger burn in his study of her, a harsh sexual tension stamped into each feature as he bent his head, and before she could stop him, possessed the taut crest of one breast with lips, tongue and finally the light edge of his teeth to devastating effect.

Her body arched instinctively, her breasts swelling and throbbing; small feminine sounds of pleasure tearing at her tense throat as a feverish heat consumed her; a pleasure she had never envisioned possible radiating out from the centre of her breast to curl tight fingers of need in her lower stomach. She wanted it all, she realised desperately; she wanted every last frisson of pleasure he could give her. Wantonly her body rejoiced in the fierce heat of his; in the complete lack of self-control.

As though sensing her feelings, he sucked fiercely on her breast, tormenting the other with urgent fingers, the fine grate of his teeth against her sensitive skin, as he gave way to savage hunger, making her shudder in frantic pleasure.

She couldn't stop him now… Hard on the heels of her admission came a fierce thrust of pleasure because the decision had been taken away from her. She wanted to give in to him, she acknowledged achingly; she wanted his possession of her body…and even though it galled her soul to admit it she knew that her love and need of him were so intense that she was prepared to take what he offered, knowing it for exactly what it was.

When he lifted his head from her breast she wanted to cry out in frustration, but gradually the tension in his body communicated itself to her and she too tensed, realising that what had caught his attention was the ringing of the telephone. As he moved away from her to answer it she was overwhelmed by a wave of sick disgust for her own behaviour. What she had been on the point of doing went against all her dearest held precepts… Even if she had been sure of his love she should not have acted so recklessly. What if he had made love to her? She could quite easily have become pregnant. The thought was sobering enough to drive out all her early need and to replace it with a sense of sick self-disgust so acute that her stomach actually twisted nauseously with it.

Something in her expression must have mirrored Piers' own feelings because when he came back from answering the phone he studied her now fully dressed body with cynical eyes, his mouth twisting derisively as he said. 'So now we know. There's nothing so potentially treacherous as sexual desire, is there? But at least I don't carry the burden of knowing I'm supposed to be committed to someone else.'

'If you mean your uncle, then I'm not,' Selina responded tensely. How could he be so calm after what had so nearly happened? Obviously men took a different view of sexual desire than women, but his cool acceptance of the fact that he had wanted her, however momentarily, surprised her.

'No, you're not are you,' he agreed sardonically. 'You realise don't you that you haven't even asked how he is, or why he is in hospital?'

'You didn't give me much chance, did you,' she reminded him curtly, impelled by an inner pain she couldn't contain to add bitterly, 'I'm surprised you can take the whole thing so lightly, I should have thought I was the last person you'd find…attractive.'

'Attractive?' He actually laughed, albeit rather cynically, 'My dear what a modest turn of phrase. "Attraction" isn't what I feel for you Selina. An almost overpowering sexual hunger is more how I'd describe it.' His precise dry voice grated on her oversensitive nerves.

'And I suppose your legal mind will soon find a means of…'

'…Reducing the problem to its component parts?' he supplied for her with a cold smile. 'My dear, I've already done so, and had vowed to give you an extremely wide berth, but tonight you caught me off-guard. Jet lag is notorious for undermining one's self-will, and I've always been very close to my uncle…'

'Meaning that what happened was my fault I suppose,' Selina was practically on the point of exploding.

'Well, you certainly didn't try very hard to stop me.'

His eyes narrowed as he took in her flushed face and angry eyes, 'And let's not forget that I'm well aware that you have some secret purpose in working for my uncle. Women have been known to use sex as a weapon before…'

Oh, but he was insufferable, to dare to suggest…but what could she say? And even if she told him the truth, would it really make any difference? He was determined to dislike and distrust her. Well then, let him. Belatedly her pride came to her rescue and she tilted her chin firmly and stared coolly at him. 'In other words, I'm still on trial,' she mocked. 'Well, be very careful, Mr Queen's Counsel, because even you are not infallible.'

'As tonight proved,' he agreed cynically, 'but don't read too much into it, will you? Whatever your relationship with my uncle is, what happened between us was simply a one off. Do I make myself clear?'

'As crystal,' Selina affirmed, wondering desperately for how long she could stop herself from being sick.

His contempt and mockery were almost more than she could bear on top of the shock of learning that her father was in hospital… Her father… Guilt flooded her as she realised she had not yet discovered exactly what was wrong with him.

'Sir Gerald,' she began formally, 'who is… what happened…?'

'Now she asks.' His smile was tormentingly unkind. 'When I arrived here this evening he was complaining of slight chest pains. Last year he had warning of a possible heart attack and was told to take things easy—hence your employ. Knowing this I insisted on ringing his doctor, who very wisely, I suspect, decided to take no chances and got him straight into hospital for some checks. That was the hospital now to say that although there's no immediate danger, they're keeping him in overnight.' He picked up his shirt, smiling sardonically as Selina averted her eyes. She had thought him a predator the first time she saw him and she knew she had been right. There was something untamed and savage about him that showed through the veneer of civilisation and she shivered slightly, knowing that something primitive deep inside herself responded to it.

'I must go.' Her voice was shaky. 'I hope Sir Gerald will be all right.' How stiff and formal she sounded, her emotions battered by Piers' love-making; her heart and body vulnerable to him.

'I'll pass on your good wishes to his family.' The cool voice dismissed her; excluding her as though from some charmed magic circle and she wanted to cry out. 'He is my father too…I have the right…' But she had no rights; her mother had abandoned those on her behalf when she had taken his conscience money. Biting her lip to stop herself from crying out her pain she headed for the door, her head held high.

It was only when she got home that the full repercussions from Sir Gerald's condition hit her. With his uncle hospitalised, Piers had every logical reason to rid himself of her. What was the point in employing a PA for a man who could not work? Sir Gerald's cases would no doubt be taken over by Piers himself as the only other QC in chambers and she would be redundant.

She woke early on Saturday morning, tense and ill at ease, longing to know how her father was and yet not daring to even try to find out. She could try and phone Piers' mother, and yet her innate sense of morality would not let her. She would not go behind Piers' back to make contact with his mother, even while her instincts told her that Dulcie would understand her need to know how Sir Gerald was.

On Saturday afternoon, still restless and

unable to settle, she set off for Hampstead Heath, telling herself that a brisk walk might help to settle her nerves.

When she got back it was beginning to go dark. Her street was deserted, a solitary car parked outside the house. The car was familiar and her pace slowed, a deep, intense excitement building up inside her. Against all logic her hopes rose. Piers had come looking for her…

Reality intruded the moment he opened the car door and stepped out. The passionate lover of the previous evening was gone and in his place was the cold, distrustful man who had first accused her of having some ulterior purpose in working for his uncle.

'So much for your supposed concern for my uncle,' he greeted her as she reached him. 'Where have you been? Cultivating another rich lover?'

The biting tone of his voice made her colour angrily. A denial trembled on her lips but she forced it back, suddenly achingly resentful that he couldn't see past his prejudices and realise the truth. Seeing the truth was supposed to be his forte and yet where she was concerned… But supposing he did see the truth…supposing he were to realise…

'I am sure you'll be relieved to hear that my uncle is not in any immediate danger.'

'Yes…yes, I am.' She turned her head away so that he wouldn't see her weak tears of relief. It was shattering to discover just how much her father had come to mean to her in so short a space of time. 'Thank you for coming to tell me.' Her voice was indistinct, muffled by the intensity of her feelings.

'My mother thought you would be concerned.'

So it had been his mother's suggestion that he come round; not his own idea. It was frightening how much that hurt.

'Of course, there's no question of him returning to chambers.'

He was enjoying twisting the knife inside her, Selina realised dully, raising pain-filled eyes to his dark face. 'Then you'll want to dispense with my services,' she said emotionlessly.

'I do,' he agreed without smiling, 'but it seems my uncle is concerned about your future—I wonder why?' The wealth of cynical contempt in his voice lashed her already tender nerves, but there was no point in retaliating. 'Do you respond as passionately to his lovemaking as you did to mine?'

'We haven't made love.' Despite all her resolves her pain burst through her self-control, her voice husky with agony as she threw the denial at him.

'You haven't? No doubt that's why he's so insistent that you go down to Dorset with him.' He registered her stunned expression and his mouth twisted in a bitter smile. 'No, I don't approve at all, but since his specialist says that on no account is he to be worried about anything, I have to give in to his wishes and transport you down there. It seems that an embargo on working is just as likely to promote a strain on his heart as doing too much, and his doctor has agreed that he can continue to work, but at a much reduced level, just as long as he does so from home. It seems that he does not consider it possible for him to do that without your valuable assistance. But let me warn you,' he added, dropping all pretence and letting her see the antagonism in his eyes, 'if you make just one step out of line, I'll have you out so fast your feet won't touch the floor. Do I make myself clear?'

Dearly as Selina longed to throw the job in his face and tell him there was no way she was going down to Dorset, she knew she could not do so. It warmed her heart to know that her father wanted her with him, even if it was only as his hard-working assistant; and she wanted to be with him too; she was greedy for all the time she had missed; she wanted her father to like and respect her. The admission made her smile wryly. She had not changed from her adolescent self so much after all...she still craved the approval and affection of her absent parent.

'Where do you go when you look like that?' There was anger in his eyes and a certain bitter resentment that made her pulses race. Fight it though he did, he couldn't entirely overcome his desire for her, but his unwilling desire was not what she wanted, and she fought back the temptation to arouse his anger to the point where he would be compelled to take her in his arms. A man who could only make love to her when he was driven beyond the limits of his self-control and who then derided himself for the weakness with bitter self-contempt was not what she wanted.

'When am I to go to Dorset?' she asked coolly, looking away from the hot anger in his eyes.

'The end of next week.' His voice was clipped, as though he were having to exercise intense self-control over himself. 'That will give you time to go through the files and assemble everything you will need in Dorset. I'll give you a list of the cases Sir Gerald will still take…'

'You'll be going to Dorset as well?'

His smile was vulpine. 'Why? If I do which are you envisaging me as, Selina? Your gaoler, or your lover?'

'Neither,' she told him shakily.

His mocking, 'Liar,' brought a surge of colour to her skin, instantly betraying her.

'I shall be joining the rest of my family there, yes,' he agreed, 'but not for another fortnight, when the summer recess begins. So don't think you'll be able to get away with anything, will you? Who knows,' he added softly, 'with time at my disposal I might even be able to find out that secret you're so anxious to conceal from me, mightn't I?'

CHAPTER SIX

WHEN Selina returned to the office after the weekend, it was to discover that everyone in the chambers seemed to have heard about Sir Gerald's heart condition.

'I half-expected something like this might happen,' Sue confessed shortly after Selina had arrived. 'I wonder what will happen now?'

Unwilling to gossip Selina said nothing. Clive Marsden, the junior barrister who normally accompanied Sir Gerald in court, also questioned her, but again she maintained a diplomatic silence.

'No doubt Piers will assume command now,' Clive commented idly. 'After all, it's been on the cards ever since he took sick. He is the natural choice, of course, but there could be some initial resentment from the older contingent.'

Although Sir Gerald and Piers were the only two Queen's Counsel in the Chambers, there were four other senior barristers, all of whom were around their middle fifties, and she could see the logic of Clive's comment.

'I doubt Mr Gresham will let that worry him.' Her voice was brittle and tense, and she wished she hadn't spoken so thoughtlessly when she saw Clive's face. 'You don't like him do you? Most unusual; the reason we don't have any female junior barristers in training here is because Sir Gerald thinks they'd spend more time spooning over his nephew than they would working—and, of course, Piers himself wouldn't want the complications it would cause.'

'How very chauvinistic—of both of them,' Selina snapped. 'Sir Gerald and Piers Gresham might both think he's God's gift to women but…'

The expression on Clive's face warned her what had happened before she swung round and found Piers watching her with ice-dark eyes that told her that he had overheard every word.

'No work to do, Miss Thorn?' he asked silkily. 'Well we'll have to do something about that won't we? For the next week you'll be working for me.' He glanced at his watch, and for a moment Selina remembered the strength and male beauty of his body without its covering of impeccable tailoring. Her body shook treacherously. 'Clive, perhaps you'd tell the other partners that I want to hold a meeting at 11.00 this morning. Anyone who can't make it can let Miss Thorn know.'

'I'm not your secretary,' Selina told him curtly when Clive had gone.

'No, we don't use them in these chambers, apart from Sue, dictating machines and a typing unit are much more effective. I'd like to see my uncle's diary, and then we'll go through all the files. He's given me a list of the ones you'll need to take with you.'

Emotion broke through her self-control as she said huskily, 'Oh you've seen him…how…'

'He is as well as many men of his age could be expected to be when he suffers from a heart condition,' he told her harshly. 'There's no need to act for my benefit,' he added, 'that limpid look of compassion and concern does not deceive me. One day I'm going to find out the truth about you, and when I do…'

'You'll use it as mercilessly against me as you do against your victims in court,' Selina threw back at him bitterly, breaking off as she saw the savage twist of satisfaction glitter in his eyes.

'So you admit it,' he said silkily, 'there is something you're hiding from me?'

In this mood he frightened her, her senses responding against her will to the compelling magnetism of his voice and eyes. She could well understand how a witness in the box must feel when confronted by him; darkly imposing in his court robes; the wig and the black silk gown which were now so familiar to her on Sir Gerald, but which were somehow threatening whenever she pictured them on Piers.

He moved towards her and she reacted in blind panic, crying out, 'Don't touch me,' as she backed away.

Her reaction was instinctive and immediately regretted, but it was too late. 'I wasn't going to,' he said coolly, adding. 'Why are you so afraid?'

'What makes you think that I am?'

His mouth twisted in cynical mockery. 'Because, my dear Selina, I can feel it, taste it, see it almost, every time I come near you.'

He was unstoppable, Selina thought half-hysterically, like some force that once unleashed could not be tamed. How different he was today from the man who had held her in his arms, his body shaking with the hunger of wanting to possess her. But then this morning he was punishing her for that hunger, she recognised intuitively and he would continue to savage her unmercifully until he felt that crime had been paid for.

'I have to appear in court after lunch. You will come with me.'

'I thought I was supposed to spend the week getting ready to join you…Sir Gerald.'

'According to my uncle you already have all his files up to date. I thought you would appreciate the experience,' he told her tauntingly. 'According to Uncle Gerald you enjoy being in court.'

'I'm surprised you're prepared to let me do anything I enjoy,' Selina thrust back at him. 'What's today supposed to be? Payment for allowing you to abuse my body?'

'Bitch!'

His eyes were so dark, they were almost black, Selina noticed feverishly as he reached for her, the bruising pressure of his mouth on hers a savage assault on her senses. She tried to withstand it; to close her mind to his brutality and anger, but something stronger than her willpower rose up inside her and her lips parted in response to his bitter demand. The heat and weight of his body against her own impelled her backwards, her hands gripping the edge of her desk. What he was doing to her made her stomach churn in sickness, her senses forced to acknowledge that this bitter, contemptuous kiss was very different from those they had exchanged before.

When he eventually released her his eyes glittered narrowly over her flushed tense face. 'That's abuse,' he told her flatly. She could feel the weight of heavy tears pressing behind her eyelids, but she dare not let them fall. Just as she started to turn her head away he gripped her chin in his fingers, forcing her to remain where she was. 'And just so that you *do* know the difference…'

She stared mutely at a point beyond his left shoulder, knowing he was not going to permit her to move and praying that her body would not betray its fear by trembling, but this time the touch of his mouth on hers was warm and gentle, its subtle pressure inducing a languor and pleasure that made her shiver tremulously. His tongue stroked her lips, parting them to taste the moist inner sweetness of her mouth. She ached to return the kiss, to press herself along the length of his body and caress him with all the feverish desire he was building inside her, but pride held her motionless, her lashes dropping to conceal any betraying emotions her eyes might reveal, as he gently released her.

'The defence rests its case.'

Selina heard him laugh as she refused to look at him. His thumb brushed across the outline of her bruised mouth and she tensed instinctively. 'You can't cross swords with me and hope to win, Selina—remember that,' he warned her softly.

She didn't move until she was sure he was gone, tensing every muscle in her body against the waves of pain threatening to break over her.

Although Selina wasn't involved in the partner's meeting she caught the shock waves when she returned to the office after lunch. Several of the girls from the typing unit were clustered in the reception area, talking in low voices when she walked in and one of them broke away from the group when she saw Selina. 'Is it true about Sir Gerald retiring and Piers Gresham taking over?' she asked Selina.

'I'm not sure if Sir Gerald actually plans to retire, but yes, at least for the present Mr Gresham will take over from him,' Selina agreed. Now that the partners had been told Sir Gerald's decision there seemed little point, to Selina's mind, in keeping the truth a secret.

'That will cause a few feathers to fly,' one of the other girls remarked acidly. 'After all, he is the youngest senior barrister in chambers.'

She was a small blonde girl whom Selina remembered Sue had once told her had set her sights on Piers when she first joined the typing unit and who, having been rebuffed, was often extremely vitriolic in her criticisms of him. At the start Selina had sympathised with her, but now she found herself saying quite sharply, 'Not at all. Mr Gresham is the only other QC in the partnership and as such must naturally take professional precedence over the others.'

'My goodness,' the blonde's eyes were speculative. 'Fallen for him have you?' The look she gave Selina was slightly malicious. 'It won't do you the slightest bit of good you know. He's strictly not in the market for any involvement with the staff. Oh no. When Mr QC Gresham decides to find a wife it will be someone from the right social class and an unblemished background.'

Selina knew the other girl was probably only giving voice to her own bitterness and yet there was a kernel of truth in what she was saying. When Piers married it would be to someone young whom he could mould and control... never the illegitimate child of his uncle's ex-secretary, she taunted herself, no matter that his uncle was also her father.

Stop tormenting yourself, she warned herself mentally as she walked through into her own office. Put him out of your mind. But with the prospect of most of the next week spent in his company that wasn't going to be easy to do.

She had seen him in court before, of course, but this was the first time she had actually accompanied him, and she could feel butterflies fluttering tensely in her stomach as she collected the case containing his wig and gown, and checked over the papers he would need. He walked into the office while she was doing so, throwing some comment over his shoulder to his junior counsel.

'Phew,' the latter complained when Piers entered his uncle's office and shut the door behind him. 'He's in a mood today. Most unlike him. I always thought he had guts of iron because nothing ever seems to move him. That's why he's so lethal in court.'

'Because he's a—human?' Selina asked wryly.

'He's prosecuting today—a particularly unpleasant hit and run. The chappie driving the car claims the mother was at fault because she wasn't watching her child, but talking to someone else.'

'And was she?'

'Yes, but Piers intends to plea that the road was a quiet suburban one leading only to the school and that the driver was in excess of the speed limit.'

'And the child?'

'Killed,' Peter Simmonds told her briefly. 'I always hate these cases; the defence will try to crucify the mother, claiming negligence on her part,' he grimaced faintly. 'With Piers in the mood he's in I don't envy the driver though. Got everything?'

When Selina nodded her head he opened the door for her. With their chambers so close to the courts it was possible to walk the intervening distance. Today the sun was shining; the weather pleasantly warm, but Selina couldn't help shivering, wondering how she would feel if she was the mother of a child who had been killed in a road accident. Guilty? Probably…but who in all honesty could not admit that it was virtually impossible to watch an active child every minute of every day…and the tragedy of life was that it only took minutes to destroy.

The mother and her solicitor were waiting for them; the mother thin and pale, her solicitor grave. While Peter Simmonds talked to them Selina stood to one side. Although she had her back to him she was aware of Piers the moment he arrived. She moved out of earshot of the small group while he discussed things with them, only to be reproved by his curt voice commanding, 'Selina come over here will you. I want to check out some of those papers you've got.'

While the men prepared for the hearing Selina sat with the mother. Her husband, she explained, could not take the time off work. 'He's already on short time,' she told her, 'and if he takes time off… I've had to leave the other two kids with his mother as it is, and she isn't best pleased about that.' Worry and pain had carved lines into her pale forehead, and although Selina guessed that she couldn't be more than twenty-seven or -eight, already she looked nearly ten years older.

'I suppose you think it's awful, me being here to get money for our Tommy's death,' she added awkwardly, 'It won't bring him back I know, but I had this little part-time job that helped out, and I've had to give that up. It's me nerves see… I can't bear to have the other two out of my sight.'

Tears weren't very far away and Selina's heart ached with sympathy for her. Poor woman. 'Just darted out into the road he did…right under me nose. I called out to him to stop… I'm always warning the kids about that road. Dangerous it is, but folks don't seem to care the way they race up and down it. There's a sports centre next to the school and there's always comings and goings… At first I thought he'd just passed out like… There was no blood you see…nothing. But then when I touched him…' she started to shake. 'I just knew somehow…I just knew… The driver was shouting at me…saying I should have been watching him, but he just slipped away…' She started to cry and Selina reached out squeezing her hand gently. What could she say? What emotion had she ever experienced that could compare with this woman's? What agony it must be to lose a child she thought help-lessly...what eternal torment.

'Mrs Evans.' Piers had come to stand beside them and for once she had not been aware of his presence. 'We'll be going into court shortly. Are you sure you feel up to it? We can ask for an ad-journment if you wish. The defence will be asking you some pretty hard questions. You remember we talked about them?'

The woman gulped and blew her nose, shaking her head fiercely. 'No...best get it over and done with. Whatever they ask me I can only tell the truth.'

Selina's heart was wrung with pity for her. The truth could present many faces and a skilled bar-rister was adept at choosing the one that best suited his case.

Once inside the courtroom, she saw a row behind the desk provided for the prosecution. Over on the other side of the room the car driver was also sitting down. With a small thrill of envy Selina saw that his barrister was a woman. How elegant she looked in her wig and gown. In other circumstances that could have been her, Selina thought wryly. Across the intervening space both sets of legal representatives acknowledged one another, and Selina noticed how the woman's expression changed as she recognised Piers.

This particular case was one of several legal aid cases the chambers handled. There was no need for a barrister of Piers' standing to involve himself in it, but Sir Gerald had once told her that it was their policy to do so, both because it was good training for the more junior barrister to see how a more senior man worked and because, as he had put it, 'In this country the cost of becoming a barrister is mitigated slightly in the initial stages by the education one can receive from the State, and that being the case I feel, and Piers agrees with me, that it is only just and fair that that cost is repaid where and when we can repay it.'

The case followed its set pattern, but it was one that Selina found endlessly fascinating, although on this occasion she could not remain as impartial as she knew she ought.

Although the defence counsel was persuasive in her plea—her questions designed to portray

Piers' client as an irresponsible mother—she was no match for Piers. In the end Selina was not surprised when the court found in their client's favour, although she was realistic enough to admit that the case could have gone either way and that they had won simply because of Piers' greater skill as a lawyer.

Piers disappeared after the case was over; presumably to change out of his robes Selina thought. Unlike even other members of their own chambers he seemed to derive no pleasure in wearing his robes outside the courtroom, and yet there was no denying that they suited him. She shivered slightly, still affected by the way he had destroyed the defence's case. The car driver, who had seemed such an unshakeable witness when questioned by his own counsel, had back-tracked and muddled his way through his evidence when attacked by Piers.

Unsure whether she was expected to wait around until Piers came back, or make her own way back to chambers, Selina hesitated. Their client turned to thank Peter yet again before being led away by her solicitor.

'Time I wasn't here,' Peter announced

glancing at his watch. 'I promised my wife, I'd try to get home early tonight.' He groaned slightly, 'My eldest's parents' night at school. Tell Piers I've gone will you?' he asked making the decision as to whether she should stay or go for her.

Ten minutes later, when Selina saw Piers sauntering down the corridor towards her, deep in conversation with the defence counsel, she wished she hadn't waited. His eyebrows lifted querying when he saw her, and Selina did not miss the way his companion's eyes mirrored faint hostility as she looked at her.

'Excuse me a second, Fiona.' He left the other woman's side and came over to her. 'Something wrong?'

Flushing as uncomfortably as a schoolgirl caught up in the toils of a crush on a more senior scholar Selina could only stare at him blankly, pulling herself together only when she saw the beginnings of a frown touching his forehead, his mouth drawing down. Dear God that pain tearing her apart must be jealousy! She had barely been able to endure the sight of that other woman at his side…

'Er…no…' Good heavens, she was stammering like a fool. 'Peter asked me to tell you he's gone home...'

His expression told her that he was less than impressed. 'Piers...I thought we were going for a drink.' Fiona's cold blue eyes flashed daggers at Selina.

'Be with you in a second. Take this back to the office for me then, will you,' he said coolly, handing Selina the case containing his court robes.

She was seething as she took it, all too conscious of the other woman's presence, and of being treated like some serving girl, there only to do her master's bidding, but she refused to let Piers see how she felt. If he did he would only gloat, she told herself bitterly, turning her back on the other couple as she walked towards the exit.

That night she was tormented by uneasy dreams. In one she was in the witness box being cross-questioned by Piers. 'Tell me the truth,' he kept demanding, his expression bitter and full of dislike for her.

In another she was tearing at the fine silk of his robes, shredding the fabric into ribbons until it turned to his flesh, taut and sleek, beneath her fingers, her nails drawing little trails of raised skin, scoring into its smoothness as she grasped him in the paroxyms of a fierce desire.

She woke up unrefreshed, haunted by vague memories of what she had dreamed, shuddering a little over them while she showered. What was happening to her? Was it really such a short time ago that she had thought herself safe from suffering human emotions; that she had thought she would work for her father and emerge from the experience unscathed? It seemed incredible now that she could have been so naive. Perhaps this was her punishment for what she was doing; that she should fall in love with Piers.

He was in Sir Gerald's office when she got there; she could hear him on the phone. 'New York,' Sue whispered confidingly as she sidled in with a tray of coffee.

New York! Did that mean he might have to fly out there? She knew very little about the case he was involved in over there, apart from the fact that the Americans were consulting him on various points of English law connected with their client's law-suit. Half of her hoped he would have to go so that she would not have to endure the daily torture of seeing him; the other half prayed that he would not.

When he thrust open the communicating door and said curtly, 'Come in here a minute will you, Selina,' she followed him mutely into the office. The desk was scattered with papers. A file on the edge of it caught her eye and her heart started to pound unevenly as she read her own name on it. 'Your personnel file,' he told her coolly, following her eyes. 'It makes interesting reading.'

'You flatter me.'

It was verbal sword play and she was like a clumsy amateur matched against an almost unmatchable skill. His smile was unkind and she tensed waiting. 'I'm just reading up on the Lockwood case,' he told her smoothly. 'It's very interesting.'

Adam Lockwood had been accused by his company of selling details of a new product they were developing to a rival firm. He had been with them for twenty-five years and had been one of their most trusted employees. His employers were their client, and his defence was that he was being blackmailed at the time by a woman he had an affair with.

'It never fails to amaze me what your sex will do in the name of that emotion they so rashly describe as love. Tell me, Selina,' he asked softly, 'what do you think of a woman who blackmails a man she's supposed to love?'

Selina wasn't deceived; she could remember what he had said to her about Sir Gerald. 'Either she's been so hurt by her lover that the only way she can ease the pain is to hit back at him, or...'

'She never loved him in the first place, but was simply using him and will continue to use him,' Piers finished for her.

'You have an extremely jaundiced view of the female sex,' Selina told him shakily.

'Do I? Realistic would have been my description. While you are staying at my uncle's home I trust you will not do anything to abuse the hospitality you will be given there,' he said abruptly, changing the conversation. 'My aunt has already suffered once through the machinations of a woman like yourself. She even looked like you,' he added broodingly, studying her with bitter eyes while Selina's heart thumped frantically.

To cover her agitation she said angrily, 'What

are you expecting me to do? Sneak into bed with Sir Gerald?'

The dark flush of colour under his skin both excited and alarmed her. She knew she had made him angry and the memory of other occasions when she had aroused that emotion in him flooded through her body, making it ache for his embrace.

'He sleeps with my aunt,' he told her tightly. 'Be warned Selina; just one step out of line while you're in Dorset and…' He cursed as the phone rang, and while he answered it Selina made her escape.

How could he think she would really… She took a deep breath trying to steady herself. He despised and disliked her and she knew if she had any sense she would seal her heart against him, but it was already too late.

She didn't see him again until lunch time when he came into her office to say curtly, 'I have to fly to New York tomorrow, and I'm not likely to be back for ten days or so. I've arranged with my mother that she'll drive you down to Dorset. She'll telephone you with all the arrangements.'

The rest of the week passed slowly, broken up

only on Wednesday afternoon when Dulcie
Gresham rang as Piers had promised.

'You'll love it at Homings,' she told Selina
when they had made their arrangements. 'I grew
up there, so perhaps I'm prejudiced.' She went
on to chat for several more minutes but all
Selina's starved senses could register when she
eventually hung up was that not once during their
conversation had his mother mentioned Piers.

She was ready and waiting at ten o'clock on the
Saturday morning when Dulcie arrived, driving
an immaculate Jaguar car.

'My goodness, you obviously believe in travel-
ling light,' she commented when she opened the
boot for Selina to put her bags inside.

'I didn't have a lot to pack,' Selina confessed.
There weren't many casual clothes in her
wardrobe, but feeling that her office suits would
look rather out of place, she had packed several
plain skirts, adding T-shirts and jeans in the hope
that she would be neither under-nor over-dressed.

'Casual gear is very much the order of the day,'
Dulcie told her glancing approvingly at the buttermilk linen skirt Selina was wearing with its
toning buttermilk and grey cotton knit sweater.

'I hope you've packed something for evening though,' Dulcie warned her. 'Mary does tend to entertain rather a lot during summer recess. I dare say she'll be keeping things rather low key this year in view of Gerald's condition, but I'm sure there will be the odd dinner party.'

'But surely I won't be expected to attend,' Selina protested. 'After all, I'll be there to work…'

'My dear, you make yourself sound like a governess invited to join the family for dinner,' Dulcie laughed. 'Of course, you'll dine with us.'

That meant she would have to go out and buy something to wear Selina reflected, thinking about the only formal dress she had included in her packing. A plain silk jersey it was attractive enough but it sounded as though she might need more than one evening outfit.

Dulcie Gresham drove well, chatting idly as she did so, wry comments about her brother's family, with the odd anecdote thrown in.

'You'll meet all the girls, but probably not at the same time. They all spend some of the summer with their parents. I think you'll find them easy enough to get on with although Helen, the youngest, can be a little reserved at first.

'We're all relying on you to stop Gerald from working too hard,' Dulcie told Selina when eventually they turned off the M4 and started meandering down winding country roads. 'This isn't the most direct route,' she confessed, 'but it saves getting snarled up in the traffic. How are you finding working for Piers?'

The question caught Selina slightly off-guard. 'Different,' she responded cautiously. Had he told his mother about his suspicions of her? Somehow she doubted it. She remembered seeing her personnel file lying on his desk. Why had he been looking at it? There was nothing there that could lead him to the truth, no real pointers to the past...that had been wiped out when the social worker had confused her real father with her mother's lover. All her file would tell him was that one Selina Thorn had been orphaned at age eleven by the death of her parents in a car crash. That those supposed parents had not been married and that her real surname was that of his uncle's ex-mistress was something he was hardly likely to uncover. Or at least she hoped it was. She gave a faint shiver as she pictured him confronting her with the truth and Dulcie Gresham noticing it said, 'Oh dear, are you cold, I'll turn the heater on.'

'I'm fine,' Selina assured her. 'Just someone walking over my grave.' The grave of all her hopes that Piers might love her as she loved him, she told herself mentally, trying to drag her thoughts way from him and concentrate instead on what lay ahead.

Homings was a gracious Tudor building set against a backdrop of gently rolling hills and their slopes wooded. A small river ran along one boundary and they had to drive over a narrow bridge to get through the gates. The garden was well-maintained, filled with a blaze of cottage flowers, the lawns smooth and green. Someone obviously expended a good deal of time and effort on it.

'The garden is Mary's baby,' Dulcie told her, guessing her thoughts, 'she works in it every spare minute.'

She brought the car to a halt in front of the house. The door opened and an excited Golden Retriever came bouncing out followed by a short plump woman with iron grey hair and a friendly, open face. She embraced Dulcie warmly, exclaiming, 'Dulcie dear, how elegant you look as always. Thank goodness the girls take after Gerald's family and not mine, otherwise I'm afraid they'd have been short-changed on looks. And this must be Selina.' She smiled at her. 'Come on inside my dear, you must be dying for a cup of tea. You can't know how relieved I am to see you. Forcing Gerald to rest has been sheer purgatory, but now that you're here, that will be your task.'

Following the other two women inside, Selina paused to admire the polished floor of the hall. A copper bowl filled with flowers sat in the centre of a polished oak table. Sunlight danced in through the mullioned windows and a sense of peace seemed to reach out and enfold her the moment she walked inside.

'Let's go into the sitting room,' Mary Harvey suggested, leading the way. 'The drawing room faces north, unfortunately,' she told Selina, 'and it always looks terribly cold and unwelcoming. I remember the first time I saw your parents was in that room,' she added to Dulcie. 'I was most fearfully scared—especially of your mother.'

'Yes. Gerald always was her favorite,' Dulcie agreed with a chuckle. 'I can remember the consternation it caused when Gerald wrote home that he intended to marry you. Our parents wanted him to qualify as a barrister before marrying, but he wasn't prepared to wait. He was afraid of losing you to someone else.'

Mary's smile was reminiscent... 'We were far too young,' she said softly. 'It's high time Piers found himself a wife,' she added in a more astringent tone as she poured tea. 'Don't you think so, Selina?'

What on earth could she say? She was prevented from having to answer by Dulcie Gresham interrupting briskly, 'I couldn't agree with you more Mary. I want my grandchildren while I'm still young enough to enjoy them. I don't suppose you'd care to take on the task, would you, Selina?' she added with a twinkle in her eyes, adding for her sister-in-law's benefit, 'Sparks seem to fly every time Selina and Piers meet... I'm not quite sure why.'

Once again Selina was saved the necessity of replying, this time by the arrival of a tall, elegant woman in her early thirties, her similarity both to Piers and his mother making the relationship instantly obvious.

'Ah, Helen my dear, come and meet Selina,' her mother smiled. 'Selina, this is my eldest daughter, Helen. She's very kindly been helping me to look after Gerald.'

'Yes…how is Sir Gerald?' Selina asked quietly, exchanging smiles with Helen. 'I wanted to telephone before, but I didn't want to intrude.'

'Nonsense,' Dulcie said briskly. 'Gerald thinks the world of you. I can't remember when he last took to someone so much, can you Mary?'

'No, I can't,' the other agreed warmly. 'You can't know what a relief it is to have someone here who can talk to him about his work and stop him from worrying. Of course he often discussed cases with Piers, but sometimes they argue, and then Gerald gets terribly upset.'

'Because both of them are too pig-headed to give in,' Helen said calmly. 'No tea for me, mother,' she interrupted as Mary started to pour an extra cup. 'I've got to go and collect the boys from their tutor.'

'How are the children? I'm looking forward to seeing them,' Dulcie asked warmly.

Helen smiled wryly. 'Not so bad. Both of them are flagging a little with their English, and having extra lessons during the holiday hasn't gone down at all well, but it's only another year until they start their "O" levels so they don't have much choice.'

When Helen finished speaking Mary told Dulcie and Selina that some friends were coming round to dinner that evening.

'They're bringing their son with them,' Mary added to Selina. 'He's newly back from Australia and recently divorced, poor man. I'm putting him next to you, Selina. I hope you don't mind my making use of you in this way. Gerald says I'm to remember you're here to help him, not to make up the numbers on my dinner table, so if you'd rather rest this evening?'

'Not at all,' Selina responded politely. She felt oddly drawn to her hostess, who seemed both genuinely warm-hearted and slightly shy. Neither glamorous nor elegant she nevertheless conveyed a warmth towards her that increased Selina's guilt at her own deception. She would never have been accepted so readily by this family if they knew the truth; that she was the daughter of the woman who had come so close to wrecking the security of their home.

'I'll show you up to your room. Dulcie you're in your usual,' Mary told her with a smile, adding to Selina. 'We've organised an office for Gerald in the room next to the one Piers normally uses when he comes here. The one good thing about this house is that at least we have plenty of space, and although Gerald normally uses the library when he works at home during the summer recess, Dr Glover thought it might be advisable if he didn't have to cope with the stairs at this stage, so I'm afraid you'll be doing a good deal of running up and down, as he keeps all his law books in the library.'

'That's what I'm here for,' Selina reassured her with a smile.

Her room was at the end of the corridor; large and prettily furnished in a traditionally patterned Sanderson paper with matching curtains and covers. It looked out over the gardens and the river and then beyond to the small village, and it was equipped with its own bathroom; a bonus she had not expected.

'We had them installed several years ago,'

Mary explained. 'Fortunately most of these rooms had their own dressing rooms which we were able to convert. I'll leave you to unpack, and if you like when you're ready I'll show you round. Gerald's sleeping at the moment. Dr Glover's prescribed a mild tranquilliser for him just for this week but he'll be anxious to see you in the morning.'

'Sir Gerald won't be at dinner then?'

A flicker of pain showed in her hostess's faded hazel eyes. 'No, I'm afraid not,' she agreed. 'Dr Glover thought it might be too much for him at this stage, although he is permitted to get up for several hours each day. He gets so bored though, poor lamb—that's where I'm hoping you'll be able to help us—keep him occupied and stop him fretting about work.'

'I'll do my best,' Selina assured her.

Now that she was here in her father's home, she wasn't sure what she felt… She liked Mary and she had been drawn to Helen, too, although she had sensed a reserve in the latter; a faint holding back, which could have been explained by her aunt's comment earlier, or which might stem from something else.

Now we had met two of her half-sisters it gave her a brief stab of pain to know that only she knew of their relationship. Doubtless if they did know they would not want to acknowledge her.

CHAPTER SEVEN

'SELINA, do come in and meet everyone.'

Mary had told her after her tour of the house that pre-dinner drinks would be served in the drawing room at seven-thirty, and she had waited several minutes after that time before going downstairs, not wanting to be the first in the room.

Helen and Dulcie she recognised, but not the man with them, who was probably Helen's husband.

Mary had been talking to another couple when Selina walked in and she left them to welcome her into the room.

It was a slightly nerve-racking sensation; being the only stranger in this roomful of old friends, but they soon put her at her ease. Richard and Sonia Vaughan were a charming couple, who she learned farmed locally, and Alex, their son, tall with sun-streaked blonde hair, was a quiet man in his late thirties with a rather shy smile and a voice that held just a tinge of an Australian accent.

Mary's other great love after her garden was cooking, Helen had told Selina before dinner, and certainly the meal she had provided for them was delicious. What a difference it made to taste home-grown, properly cooked vegetables, Selina marvelled, comparing their flavour to those she normally bought at her local supermarket. Although initially shy, Alex proved to be an amusing companion. He had come home to take over the management of his parents' farm, he explained to Selina over their main course. 'With a failed marriage behind me it made sense to have a fresh start.' His voice was faintly bitter and Selina was instantly sympathetic, sensing that he had not yet come to terms with the loss of his wife.

'The only good thing is that we didn't have any children,' he added. 'Melanie, my wife, didn't want them. She thought they would interfere with her career. You work for Sir Gerald I understand,' he commented, changing the subject and smiling wryly. 'I'm afraid I'm becoming something of a divorce bore.'

'Not at all. It's only natural to want to talk about it. I'm afraid we British as a rule tend to bottle up our feelings too much.'

'Umm. I'm not altogether in favour of discussing one's private business at the drop of a hat, but there's something about you that encourages one to confide in you. You have a very sympathetic smile. I believe you'll be staying here for most of the summer?'

'That's the plan at the moment,' Selina concurred.

'Then I wonder if you'd allow me to take you out for dinner one evening? I promise I won't talk about my divorce all night if you agree,' he added smiling at her.

Sensing that he would be hurt if she refused Selina said cautiously, 'I'd like that very much, but as yet I'm not sure what my routine will be while I'm here, so could we leave it until I'm settled in?'

'Of course, although I suspect once it gets around that there's a beautiful blonde living in the area, I'll have to stand in line for my date,' he said ruefully.

After dinner they returned to the drawing room

to chat and drink coffee, and once again Selina found she was made very welcome within the small, intimate circle of family and friends. At one point she found herself chatting to Helen and her husband Mike. Dulcie had described Helen as the most reserved of the sisters.

'We're all so relieved that you agreed to come down here,' she told Selina as they drank their coffee. 'Daddy's done nothing but sing your praises since you went to work for him. He says you're wasted working as a mere PA and we all feel that now that you're here to take charge of his precious files, he'll be able to relax a bit more. What made you choose to work in a barrister's chambers?' she added curiously. 'I mean, they pay their staff notoriously poorly, and with your skills surely industry…'

'I've always been fascinated by the law,' Selina broke in quickly. 'I would have loved to train for the bar, but as I was saying earlier, financially it just wasn't possible.'

'No, of course not, Daddy was telling us that you were orphaned very young.'

Helen's ready sympathy made Selina feel acutely uncomfortable. She hated the way she was having to deceive these people and yet what else could she do. How would they feel if they knew the truth? They certainly wouldn't want to make her welcome among them then! The habit of concealing the details of her birth was so ingrained in her that normally she rarely gave it a second thought, but now, suddenly, it was being brought home to her just exactly what she was doing.

WHEN Selina was summoned to Sir Gerald's presence the next morning it was to find him sitting up in a large leather chair, in the room adjacent to his bedroom, which had been turned into a study for him, looking so fit and well that Selina found it almost impossible to believe that he had virtually just come out of hospital.

'There's no need to look at me like that,' he told her dryly, 'I won't melt. All this fuss and bother...' He gave a brief snort. 'Ridiculous... these doctors, nothing but a load of old women... Now, let's get down to some work.'

Despite his assertion that there was absolutely nothing wrong with him, Selina soon discovered that he tired fast, even though he did not want to admit it. Pain and love mingled inside her as she watched him. He was her father and she had come to care for him with a depth she would never have thought possible. She ached for the relationship with him that she had been denied and yet was logical and fairminded enough to admit that it was probably better that she, one child, should have suffered, especially as she had never known him as a father, than that three other children should have been robbed of a parent.

'You're looking very pensive, something wrong?'

She shook her head and smiled briefly, taking advantage of his concern to say lightly, 'I'm just tired…the drive down here yesterday wore me out.'

The grey eyebrows rose, but he made no comment, instead dismissing her with the advice that she go and stretch her legs. It was close to lunch time but still within the two hours Mary had warned her was all Sir Gerald's doctor was going to allow him to spend on work each day.

He didn't join the rest of the family for lunch and Mary was also missing.

'Mother is having lunch upstairs with Daddy,' Helen explained with a smile. 'She adores him and always has done…too much I sometimes think… What will you do with the rest of your day?'

'I've got some phone calls to make for Sir Gerald and some information to dig out, so I think I'll take myself off to the library after lunch and get on with it in there.'

'Well, do try to join us at four for a cup of tea. We don't expect you to work every hour God sends while you're here you know. We'll be more than happy if you can just keep Daddy from exhausting himself.'

A week passed in the same leisurely, relaxed fashion as the first day. Selina was now familiar with both the layout of the house and its gardens; she had driven into the nearby town and explored its narrow medieval streets and the ruins of its once proud castle. Dulcie had returned to London and the doctor had called and had pronounced himself pleased with his patient's progress.

She should have been pleasantly content Selina acknowledged, but she wasn't. Seeing her father against the background of his home and family had aroused all the envy she had known as a child, although in a much milder vein and her heart ached as she wondered if he ever spared a thought for her; the child he had fathered but never known. Why should he, she told herself sternly; he didn't want you...you weren't conceived with his consent...you were conceived because your mother wanted to use you to force his hand...why should he spare you any thoughts...any time...any emotion.

She found her self-inflicted misery so depressing that when Alex Vaughan telephoned and asked her out to dinner she accepted.

'Marvellous. I'll pick you up around eight, if that's okay with you?'

It was, and although Selina had had all her evenings free since her arrival at Homings, she nevertheless checked with Mary that it would be all right for her to be out that night.

'My dear of course it's all right,' her hostess told her. 'I'm so glad you're going out. I feel terribly guilty because it must be so dull for you down here, away from London.'

'Not at all, I love it,' Selina told her truthfully. 'I feel guilty because I'm doing so little work.'

'You're stopping Gerald from over-tiring himself and exhausting his nervous energy worrying about work,' Mary told her quietly, 'and I can't tell you what a relief that is to me. You go out on your date and enjoy yourself. I'll leave the front door unlocked for you, so don't worry about getting in at any particular time. Alex Vaughan is a nice boy, although I never took to his wife… Poor Alex, I think he was rather dazzled by her; she was extremely beautiful, but definitely not cut out to be a farmer's wife.'

Selina wasn't sure where Alex intended taking her, and since Mary insisted she was to have the afternoon off, she decided to drive into Meltham to see if she could find a new outfit dressy enough for evening wear and a dinner date without being too fussy.

She found what she was looking for in a small boutique down a narrow side street. A misty lilac-blue silk dress with thin shoe string straps and a slim skirt that clung lovingly to her hips and thighs. The jacket that went with it added a touch of formality that she welcomed, and it was an added bonus to discover that because it was in a small size the price had been marked down slightly. It wasn't like anything else she had in her wardrobe, being far more frivolous and feminine than the clothes she normally bought. It suited her though, and on some impulse she couldn't define she went into a hairdressers she had noticed on her first visit to the town and had her hair shaped and layered into a style that allowed her to retain its length while encouraging it to curl slightly—something that its previous heaviness had prevented.

The stylist complimented her on its sheen and colour adding that he had very few clients with such naturally fair hair. Selina had always thought it insipid. She would have preferred to have been dark. She trembled slightly, suddenly remembering the thick, soft feel of Piers' hair beneath her fingers. Piers. He was never out of her thoughts. When was he coming back from New York? When would she see him again? What did it matter? She had no future with him...he didn't love...couldn't love her.

ALEX called for her at eight as he had promised, his eyes lighting up appreciatively when she opened the door for him.

'How very lovely you look,' he told her as he opened the passenger door of his car for her.

Selina had been dubious about wearing the new dress, but in the end had given in to the feminine impulse to do so and was glad she had when Alex drew up in the forecourt of what she guessed had once been a private family home and was now a hotel.

'At weekends they have dinner dances here, but when I telephoned they were fully booked, hence the invitation for tonight,' he explained as they walked in. 'I haven't dined here before, but I've been told it's very good.'

It was. The restaurant was elegant and yet relaxing; the atmosphere intimate without being overdone. The nouvelle cuisine food they were served was mouthwateringly delicious and Selina enjoyed every mouthful.

Once he had relaxed a little Alex was a pleasant companion. He talked a little about his life in Australia in general terms and Selina learned that he had worked on one of the huge sheep stations as a manager.

'I met Melanie while I was on holiday in Sydney. She was working for a PR firm there.' His eyes darkened with pain and he became quiet. 'I'm sorry to bore you with all this,' he said at last. 'I don't think I've come to terms with it in my own mind yet.'

'These things take time.' Selina offered the platitude with a bright smile, knowing that no amount of time could ever lessen the pain of loving Piers.

It had been a pleasant evening, but she was not entirely unhappy when it was over. Alex came with her to the front door after he had stopped the car and hesitated a moment in its porch, their shadows intermingling in the moonlight as they stood close together, his fair head bent over hers.

'I've enjoyed tonight. I have to go away for several weeks, but when I come back,' he said quietly, 'could we do it again?'

Sensing his loneliness, Selina nodded her head. 'I'd like that.'

'You're very kind.' He bent his head and brushed her lips with his; the salutation of a friend; no more than a brief 'thank you' for her time and sympathy, but when the door opened behind them and they were caught in a brilliant blaze of lights Selina jumped back as guilty as a teenager caught in her very first passionate kiss.

'Hello, Alex.'

The familiar timbre of the male voice sent shivers of reaction running down her spine. Piers was back!

In a daze she listened to Alex wishing Piers a 'good night', stepping back automatically into the house when Piers held the door open for her.

He closed it behind her and then said sardonically, 'You don't waste much time do you? You realise that he's married?'

'Divorced actually.' She was too stunned to do more than defend herself as an automatic reflex action. 'When did you arrive?'

'Half an hour ago. I was just on the point of going to bed when I saw the car drive up. Where did he take you?'

'Just out to dinner.'

'Sorry I interrupted your romantic good nights.'

He didn't sound sorry at all, but Selina refrained from responding.

IT was the end of her brief interlude of peace. Piers' arrival seemed to change everything. When she went in to Sir Gerald in the mornings Piers was invariably there, his cool, watchful eyes following her every movement, warning her that he was just waiting for her to slip, to make that one fateful mistake that he could pounce on. Mealtimes with him present were an ordeal because all the time she was conscious of his presence, of the power of his personality reaching out to threaten her. She loved him and was desperately afraid of betraying that love because she feared if she did he would use it to destroy her. Looking into his cold eyes she found it almost impossible to believe that they had once burned with hot desire for her. Now that desire was gone or held in such strong control that she would never see it again.

'You seem to have an extraordinary effect on my nephew,' Sir Gerald commented wryly one afternoon having witnessed a brief exchange of words between them.

'We don't get on very well,' Selina told him, avoiding looking at him.

'Oh, is that what it is?' His voice was mild, but something told Selina that he was amused. 'That's an achievement in itself,' he told her when she finally forced herself to look queryingly at him. 'Piers does not normally concern himself enough with other people to the extent of "not getting on".'

'Sometimes it happens that two people are naturally antipathic.'

'So it does.'

Nothing else was said, but Selina was conscious of Sir Gerald watching them with mild and amused curiosity whenever they were together. She felt as though her control was being stretched to breaking point, her nerves so tense that the slightest thing could overset them.

On the Sunday Helen and her family left. Selina was sorry to see them go. She liked her youngest half-sister, just as she had liked her eldest.

Without them the house was quiet. In the afternoon Piers drove off in his car after lunch, without saying where he was going, leaving Mary and Selina alone in the drawing room. When the former excused herself to go upstairs and sit with her husband, who was still forbidden to come downstairs until dinner time, Selina got up and wandered into the study intending to do some work on one of Sir Gerald's cases, ready for him to check on Monday morning.

It was while she was there that her eyes were drawn to the family photographs adorning the large mahogany desk. She was studying them silently when Mary appeared and explained that she was just going to take Sir Gerald for a run in the car.

'He's itching to get out and capable of taking himself if I don't give in and take him. We shan't be long.' She smiled adding, 'I hope you don't mind us deserting you like this.'

Selina shook her head, summoning a smile for her hostess. In point of fact for some reason today she felt decidedly low… What she felt was that she was an outsider looking in on an enviably happy family life, she told herself hardily, and she *was* an outsider. All at once she became obsessed by a need to know if her father had ever thought about her at all during the years of her growing up…if he had ever treasured any little thing just to show that he acknowledged her existence. Almost before she knew what she was doing, she was giving in to a compulsion so strong that she could not resist it; sliding open the desk drawer where Mary had told her they kept the old family photographs.

The top album was the most recent; containing photographs of the Ruby Wedding. Selina poured the longest over one of Piers, her heart aching for the impossibility of her feelings for him.

Once started it was impossible for her to stop. Ignoring the inner voice that told her what she was doing was wrong she flicked back page after page, going back through the years to the time when the girls had been small. Deeply engrossed in what she was doing she never heard the library door open; never became aware of the grim-faced man towering over her until he wrenched the album out of her fingers, his voice harsh with bitterness as he exclaimed.

'Just what the hell do you think you're doing, or has my aunt given you her permission to go through her private things?'

Piers! Guilty colour flared up under her skin.

'What was in your grubby little mind I wonder to motivate you to invade someone's privacy and violate their trust in the way you were doing? What were you hoping to find?'

'You don't understand.' Scrambling to her feet Selina faced him bravely.

'On the contrary I understand all too well,' he told her thickly, 'but before I throw you out into the gutter where you belong I intend to find out exactly what you thought you were doing. Come with me.'

Grasping her wrist, he tugged her towards the

door. Selina tried to stop him, panic flooding through her body. 'Stop it, you're hurting me,' she complained.

He turned on her, his lips curled back in a feral smile, his eyes glittering with an emotion she could only assume was hatred.

'Not half as much as I'd like to,' he told her grimly. 'Now come with me.'

She didn't want to; she wanted to resist the force of his contemptuous anger and withstand it, but his strength was the greater, his threat to pick her up and carry her forcing her to accede to his demand.

When he eventually stopped outside the room she knew to be his she panicked, fighting against him with all her strength, gasping with pain as he shouldered open the door and pulled her inside with little regard for the bruises he was inflicting on her tender skin.

Once inside he slammed the door shut with his foot, refusing to let her go. 'Now then...' He was breathing heavily, his chest rising and falling unevenly beneath his jacket and shirt. 'Let's just see if we can't find out what all this is about shall we?'

His attitude of open contempt was so infuriating that Selina reacted instinctively, throwing her head back defiantly and bracing herself against his grip, fighting to break free.

'I have nothing to say to you,' she hissed at him, 'and nothing you do to me will make me speak.'

'Is that a fact?'

A brilliant fever of anger seemed to burn in his eyes. 'Still sure you've nothing to tell me?'

Fighting to hold the bitterness of his scrutiny Selina shook her head, gasping out loud as his fingers tightened briefly into her skin before he released one hand to tangle his fingers in her hair, pulling her head back with almost painful ferocity, so that the slim line of her throat was arched back, her face tense with distrust and fear. As he bent his head slowly towards her she could feel that tension spreading right through her body. She badly wanted to pull away; to close her eyes to blot out the dangerous bitterness of his, but movement was impossible. She seemed to be held fast; mesmerised almost by the powerful emotions emanating from him. He stopped a whisper away from her lips.

'Tell me the truth.'

Selina swallowed hard, the muscles in her throat contracting painfully. She shook her head, her moaned protest silenced by the heat and pressure of his mouth possessing hers. Piercing darts of panic lanced through her, her body tensing against the male pressure of his as Piers released his hold on her arm, instead sliding his hand over the bunched muscles of her back, and down to her waist where it clamped her against the hard outline of his own body.

His mouth on hers was hot and fierce, not coldly contemptuous as she had anticipated. She could feel her senses responding to him, her eyes wide open as she stared into his and watched as anger gave way to passion, her own nerve endings responding to the need she could see reflected in his rapidly darkening irises.

The initial reason for him bringing her here to his room was forgotten as her heart took up a slow, drum-beat thud, the blood coursing hotly through her veins as she became aware of the tension in his body, her own registering the reason for it; the need she could see burning fiercely in his eyes as he looked back at her. She stared at the lean, tense planes of his face; the

smooth tanned column of his throat before it disappeared below the crispness of his shirt and her
fingers ached to reach out and touch him; to
caress the hard maleness of his body.

Almost as though he had read her mind, he
released her briefly to wrench off his jacket and
tie, one hand returning to slide through her
tangled hair and cup the back of her skull with
fingers that stroked and massaged where before
they had punished, the other tearing impatiently
at the buttons of his shirt, laying bare a tanned
vee of flesh.

'Kiss me.'

It was a command that exerted a far more dangerous pull on her senses than any of his earlier
ones. Like someone in a dream Selina arched her
head back against the firm pressure of his hand,
her mouth parting softly as she lifted her arms,
her fingers stroking tentatively along his shoulders and up into the nape of his neck. The hoarse
sound of pleasure he made deep in his throat
sent ripples of response thrilling through her, her
whole body coming instantly alive as he took the
parted softness of her mouth with a fierce
hunger, kissing her with an abandon that made

her mind reel and her body ache for complete fulfilment.

Somehow her hands had found their way inside his shirt and were caressing the satin smoothness of his skin, her body weak and pliant as he moulded it against his own. Little shudders of pleasure raced through her as his hand found her breast, caressing it wantingly. When Piers unfastened the buttons of her blouse and laid bare the pale creaminess of her skin she felt no shame, only intense feminine pleasure in the way he studied her breasts. Dark colour filled his face and she felt the savage tremor that racked his body as he bent his head and touched his mouth lightly to the creamy flesh just above the lacy barrier of her bra. His touch fired a wild explosion of need inside her, her stomach tensing on a wave of pleasure, all restrain forgotten as her body leapt to respond to him.

Selina felt him tremble as he pushed aside the delicate cup of her bra. An aching tension filled her, her breath held as she waited yearningly for the burning touch of his mouth against her skin, but instead the lacy barrier was slipped back in place.

Shivering with reaction, Selina made to move

away from him, but Piers stopped her, grasping both her wrists in one hand, the other cupping her face so that she could not turn away from him. This was it… He was going to mock her for desiring him…he was going to reject her so humiliatingly that she would never, ever recover… he had guessed how she felt about him.

But when she looked bravely at him Selina saw that his face was still suffused with the dark flush of passion she had seen earlier, his eyes hot and hungry as he studied her pale face.

'I want to see all of you,' he told her thickly. 'To see you…to taste you…dear God, I want you as I've never wanted any other woman.'

He paused and when she said nothing he picked her up bodily with a harsh exclamation of pleasure, carrying her over to his bed. She should resist, Selina knew that. She should tell him that she wanted to leave; that she didn't want his lovemaking, but it would be a lie. Her body ached to know him as its lover, and a traitorous voice inside her warned insidiously that if she refused him now she would regret it all her life, and that at least this way she would have her memories of him.

As he laid her on the bed, the tenderness in his touch almost made her cry. Gone was the savage anger that had been in his face when he caught her inside the open desk drawer; that man might never have been.

With gentle hands he slid away the barriers of her clothes, pausing once to study the full curves of her breasts, dark colour running up under his skin as he bent his head to annoint each one delicately with his mouth. Powerless to prevent the shiver of delight that tensed her body, Selina glanced pleadingly up at him, but he shook his head slightly, his fingers not quite as steady as he removed the remainder of her clothes.

She felt no shame or embarrassment in her nudity; rather an intense feminine pride that her body could provoke the fierce response she could see glittering in his eyes and feel in the hard tension of his body as he reached out and stroked his fingers lightly from her breast to her thigh.

'Now it's your turn. Undress me, Selina,' he demanded thickly. 'I want to feel your hands against my skin.'

Like someone in a dream she complied without even thinking about it, her eyes soft and dreamy as she slid her fingers inside his shirt and then down to the few still-fastened buttons.

When she tugged his shirt free of his trousers her fingers grazed his skin and she thrilled to his harshly indrawn breath. He was lying on his side beside her, his head propped up on one elbow, studying her body with a feverish hunger that made her tremble. With shaking fingers she pushed his shirt back off his shoulders, watching him shrug quickly out of it, with eyes that were unknowingly dark with mingled excitement and awe. Reacting instinctively to the sight and proximity of him she reached out to touch him, tracing a tentative, delicate caress along his shoulder and down along the dark arrowing of hair that disappeared beneath his belt.

She felt his body clench beneath her touch and heard his harsh breathing. When she looked up into his face his eyes were closed, his mouth a tight line of urgency.

'Stop playing with me.' It was more of a groaned plea than a command but Selina reacted immediately to it, her fingers trembling so much over the buckle of his belt that in the end he had to do it for her, the sound made by his zip as he eased it down grating harshly against her ears in the thick silence of the room. He discarded the rest of his clothes with the same tense speed with which he had shrugged off his shirt and in the light from the uncurtained windows Selina saw that his body was as totally male as she had imagined. Fine dark hairs shadowed the tanned leanness of his thighs, her eyes sliding nervously away from the evidence of his arousal, but when he reached out and cradled her against his body she shuddered pleasurably at the sensation of his hardness pressing against her. His hand moved down the curve of her spine pressing her more intimately against him, the contact with his body making her shiver restlessly.

Almost without realising what she was doing Selina turned her head into the hard curve of his shoulder, first her mouth and then her teeth finding the warmth of his skin. She felt the tense stillness of surprise hold him for a moment as she tasted the warm male salt of his skin, giving in to her own growing need to touch and caress him and then when her tongue touched tentatively against the skin she had kissed he muttered her name thickly, wrenching her round in his arms, so that his mouth could fasten on hers and plunder it with a fierce heat that left her melting against him, formless clay to be moulded into whatsoever he desired.

His hands cupped her breast as it had done before, but this time there were no barriers between her sensitive skin and the probing exploration of his thumb. She shuddered deeply in pleasure, her nipples throbbing peaks of desire that shamelessly demanded his touch. The pressure of his mouth against hers softened slightly, his tongue stroking the moist outline of her lips, his free hand capturing one of hers and drawing it against his body, coaxing her to touch him with an intimacy that made him shudder deeply, her body filled with a strange, wild excitement that she could affect him so intensely with just the lightest touch. The knowledge made her bold, when his mouth left hers to explore the delicate arch of her throat, and then explore the narrow fragility of her shoulder bones, to turn her own lips into the warmth of his skin, opening her mouth to taste the maleness of it, so lost in her own tactile voyage of exploration that it wasn't until she heard his harsh gasp of pleasure that she realised that Piers had stopped kissing her and that he was lying in her arms with his eyes closed, his body throbbing its message of need into her own. As though he sensed her confusion, he muttered without opening his eyes, 'Don't stop... I want you to touch me all over, Selina... I want to feel your hands and mouth against my skin, like this...'

He bent his head, his hand cupping her breasts, his tongue painting delicate circles of delight round first one erect nipple and then the other, until she trembled in aching need, winding her fingers into his hair. His hands moulded and shaped the swollen fullness of her breasts, his breath exploding on a harsh sound of pleasure as Selina arched upwards, inviting him to taste and pleasure the deep pink buds of flesh he had aroused. His mouth burned against her skin, the grate of his teeth against the sensitive flesh a fierce throb of delight.

When his mouth sucked rhythmically on the tender crest of her breast Selina felt pangs of aching need spread out from it to the pit of her stomach, her whole body aching with need for him, the small whimpers of pleasure she couldn't stem, filling the silence of the room. When Piers released her breasts, returning to plunder her mouth, she clung eagerly to him, her hands stroking down over his body, her hips writhing instinctively against the hard pressure of his. When his hands slid from her waist to her bottom, holding her intimately against him, she gasped in aching need, pressing moist kisses along the column of his throat, feeling the muscles ridge beneath her mouth. His hand, caressing the smooth line of her thigh, made her ache with longing for his possession.

When he moved away from her, she shivered in intense disappointment, instinctively fearing his rejection, reaching up towards him and scattering impassioned kisses against his shoulders and chest. When her mouth brushed the hard nub of his nipple he muttered her name rawly, winding his fingers into her hair and imprisoning her against his body. His 'God yes…touch me there,' made her pulses race in feverish excitement, her tongue brushing tormentingly against the hard nub of flesh until he cried out, gripping the soft skin of her upper arms, his body shuddering convulsively as she repeated her caress against his other nipple.

Lost in her sensual exploration of his body, Selina was dimly aware of his hand stroking delicately along her inner thigh, but when he touched her more intimately, caressing the inner core of her femininity, pleasure exploded inside her, her teeth biting passionately into his skin, her hand finding his hard maleness and caressing it tentatively at first and then more urgently as Piers ignited in her body a wild feverish need to be filled completely by the maleness of him.

The touch of his mouth against her inner thigh made her shudder with renewed pleasure, even whilst she tried to push him away; shy of the intense intimacy of his caress.

'Your skin feels like silk.' The warmth of his breath against her body sent tiny thrills of pleasure darting through her. She loved him so much… An aching pain dragged inside her and she shivered, but not in passion this time. Piers *didn't* love her. Where it had been soft and pliant her body was now strangely stiff and resistant.

'What's wrong?'

She could see Piers frowning slightly as he released her. Her tongue seemed to have swollen in her mouth, making it impossible for her to speak. How could she explain that she loved him and that because of that the thought of him making love to her simply to appease his desire was suddenly almost nauseating? She wanted him to want her for the same reason she wanted him. What she wanted was something she would never have, she told herself sardonically, but it was impossible to recapture her earlier mood... her intense sexual desire was gone, leaving in its place a deep sense of self-revulsion.

She shivered beneath the oppressive weight of it, as Piers released her and then turned to study her. All desire had fled from his face too, his eyes starkly bitter. 'I don't know what sort of game you think you're playing,' he began, pulling on his trousers, and throwing her own clothes towards her, 'but...' His head turned sharply towards the door, his forehead creasing in a frown. Like someone turned to stone, Selina grasped her clothes protectively in front of her as the door swung open and her father walked inside, coming to an abrupt halt as he realised that Piers was not alone.

He must have said something to Piers, but Selina was too heart-sick and filled with self-disgust to register what it was. The moment they were alone and the door closed, she turned on Piers, her face as white as her underclothes, her eyes blazing with a bitterness she didn't bother to hide as she said tensely, 'I suppose you planned that didn't you… You wanted him to see me like this…to…'

'To what?' Piers was now as angry as she was herself, his mouth compressed in a cruelly savage line. 'To realise that he isn't your only lover? Why did you let me take you to bed, Selina? Fancied a second string to your bow did you, and didn't anticipate being caught with me by your other lover? Get out,' he told her thickly. 'Get out of here before I throw you out.'

He turned his back on her while she pulled on her clothes, with fingers that were suddenly numb. Her embarrassment at being faced with Sir Gerald in such an obviously compromising situation had simply been that of any daughter found in bed with her lover by her father, but Piers had totally misread the reasons behind her emotional outburst. Bitterness welled up inside her. Let him think what he wished about her… She didn't care any longer… She didn't care about anything any longer. Knowing only that she couldn't bear to stay in the house a moment longer, she fled from Piers' room and headed down the narrow flight of back stairs into the garden.

CHAPTER EIGHT

THE heat outside was oppressive, but Selina ignored it, wandering feverishly into the more remote parts of the garden. More than anything else she wanted to escape; to close her eyes and find herself back in her own small flat…back in time, in fact, to before she had ever contemplated going for that fateful interview. If she could only have that time over again how differently she would react. She shivered suddenly despite the heat. How could she face Piers after what had happened between them? How could she face her father?

She would have to face them, she told herself bitterly; and since that was the case she might as well face them as bravely as she could. Piers could not have made his lack of love for her more clear if he had shouted it from the rooftops, what in another man might have been excused on the grounds of intense jealousy could only, in him, be another indication of his contempt for her. How could he believe she could respond to him as passionately as she had done and yet still be involved with Sir Gerald?

Sick at heart she retraced her steps towards the house, slowing tensing when she saw Piers standing by the door she had come through, a deep frown creasing his forehead. Her pulse rate increased in direct ratio to her slowing footsteps, her heart thumping heavily. What was Piers doing here? Surely not waiting for her? Moistening dry lips Selina forced herself to move forward. Piers saw her and just for a moment the expression in his eyes puzzled her, but he masked it quickly, his voice almost curt as he demanded. 'What the hell was all that about?' He reached over to grasp her arm, but she evaded him, sliding sideways past him and into the house, welcoming the footsteps on the narrow stairs that warned him that they were not alone.

'Ah Selina, my dear, there you are.' Mary beamed at her, apparently completely oblivious to the tension in the atmosphere. 'Gerald was just asking where you were.'

'I'll go up to him now.' Much as she dreaded
the embarrassment of facing her father, anything
was better than standing here and being forced
to endure any more of Piers' insults.

Sir Gerald smiled warmly as she walked into the
room, his smile fading a little as he took in her
pallor, and the bruised vulnerability of her eyes.

'Selina, my dear, come and sit down.'

When she shook her head and moved instead
to the desk, picking up the nearest file, bending
her head so that the smooth fall of her hair hid
her expression from him, he added quietly,
'Please do not be embarrassed—if anyone was
at fault it was me. I should have known better
than to simply barge in like that.'

There was a moment's silence when Selina
could not bear to look at him and then she heard
him say diffidently, 'Selina, please don't think
I'm interfering, or in any way disapproving, but
you've come to mean a good deal to me in the
short time we've known one another…in a purely
avuncular fashion, I hasten to add,' he inserted
holding up his hand to prevent Selina from
speaking. 'Are you in love with my nephew?'

The question was so unexpected that for a

moment Selina didn't know what to say. 'Why should I be,' she asked a little bitterly at last. 'He isn't in love with me.'

'My dear, any fool, even an old fool like me, can see that you're not the sort of girl who spends her life hopping in and out of young men's beds. There is an air about you that is, for lack of a better description, almost virginal.' This time his smile was faintly wry. 'You'll have to forgive me for speaking to you like a Dutch Uncle, but in a way I feel responsible for what has happened.' He frowned slightly, 'It's just that Piers normally confines his romantic pursuits to women rather more sophisticated than you are yourself. I know I shouldn't interfere… I don't know why I am doing really, except that I was hurt very badly myself once and I'm fond enough of you not to want to see you going through what I endured. Piers hasn't had a very easy life,' he added abruptly. 'He lost his father at a very early age and then something happened which scarred him badly and for which I fear I'm very much to blame.' He turned slightly away from her as though faintly embarrassed and Selina felt her heart start to pound unsteadily. Instinct told her that she was about to discover the truth about his involvement with her mother and she held her breath, uncertain as to whether or not she wanted him to go on.

'It's no great secret that many years ago I was involved with another woman—it made front-page headlines at the time, although I doubt you will be able to remember them, you couldn't have been much more than a baby, if that. I thought myself so deeply in love that nothing else mattered save being with this other woman. My wife knew of my affair—I didn't make any attempt to hide it from her. Our marriage had been a good one; indeed a happy one...we had three lovely daughters, and our life together had fallen into a comfortable pattern. I was nearly forty—just a little older than Piers is now, and he was, oh, about eight I suppose. After his father's death he looked to me as the main male figure in his life, and I was very fond of him, for his own sake, not just because he was my sister's child. In many ways I suppose Piers is the son I never had. He looked up at me...hero-worshipped me in a way I suppose. He was away at boarding school at the time and in a moment of self-conceit I've long since regretted I took the woman I was involved with down to the school with me one weekend. We took Piers out to lunch, and it pleased me to see how easily my ladyfriend charmed him, here at least was one member of my family who wasn't turning against me, or so it seemed at the time.

'What cruel fools men can be when they deceive themselves. It wasn't the only visit we paid Piers... His school was in the Yorkshire Dales with a delightful hotel nearby... I didn't intentionally draw him into what was happening, but he was drawn in...and I suspect just as I was besotted so was he in his own boyish way, but of course he didn't realise the real nature of our re-lationship. She was just a friend of mine whom he'd met. I didn't swear him to secrecy or anything like that. It didn't seem necessary, and when my sister came to see me and asked that I didn't go to see him again unless I was on my own, it took some time for me to realise what had happened, and that Piers had written to his mother in all innocence telling her about my friend and how charming she was. When she found out she was bitterly furious. She'd make the little sneak sorry, she told me. I'd never seen her like that before. It shocked me... brought me back to reality perhaps, I don't know.'

Selina could well imagine her mother's reaction. She had never liked losing an admirer no matter how young or how old. Her heart contracted with pity for Piers, her love for him making it easy for her to picture the idealistic boy he had been... Oh, how her mother would have revelled in that childish hero-worship and how furious she must have been at Piers' innocent betrayal.

'Unknown to me she went up to the school... She had been there before with me and the headmaster at first saw nothing wrong in permitting her to take Piers out for the afternoon. It was only later when the boy returned alone, obviously shocked and distressed, that he telephoned me and I discovered what had happened.

'Of course I tackled her about it the moment she arrived back in town. "Someone had to tell the little brat a few home truths," was all she would say in response to my questions and when I eventually got to talk to Piers he wouldn't say a word about what had happened. My guess is that she was cruelly unkind to him, and I suspect that incident has cast a shadow over all his involvements with your sex. I don't think he's ever truly come to terms with her cruelty…. Of course when he realised the truth he was doubly bitter. He felt that by allowing himself to be bedazzled by her he had betrayed my wife and his cousins…it took him a long time to come to terms with what had happened just as it did me…'

'You parted from this woman then?' Selina didn't know how she managed to ask the question. Her mouth was dry with tension, a deep inner need to know if he had ever given a thought to her all through the intervening years over-riding her sympathy for Piers momentarily.

'Yes…but not without a good deal of heart-searching. You see by this time she was carrying my child. In those days abortions were illegal, and even if one could have been procured, I doubt I would have been able to accede to the destruction of my own child.'

'But you don't…you don't see her at all?'

If he had noticed her slip in betraying her knowledge of the sex of his illegitimate child, he obviously wasn't going to mention it. His voice

was taut with tension as he said slowly, 'No…
No…we…that is her mother and I decided that
it was best for her sake if there was no contact
between us. Besides I owed it to my wife and
existing family to cause them as little additional
pain as possible. I had already hurt them so
much… At the time it seemed the most sensible
thing to do…to give up all claim to her…'

'Have you ever regretted it?' Selina's voice
was husky; fraught with deep tension. Neither of
them seemed to be aware of the intensely
personal nature their conversation had taken;
both of them too involved in what they were
feeling to speak dishonestly.

'Many times… Every time I look at a pretty
girl like you Selina I wonder about my own
child…if she hates me…if she thinks of me at
all…if she even knows that I exist, and I pray that
if she does she forgives me…'

'For what? Giving her life?' As the words of
comfort left her lips, Selina knew suddenly,
blindingly, that she meant them; that all her bitterness was gone, washed away in the sure flood
of knowledge that thanks to this man she possessed the great gift of life…

She was healthy; intelligent and free…what greater gifts could any father give his daughter? It was as though a huge burden had suddenly been lifted from her shoulders. She felt tears sting her eyes and brushed them away with the back of her hand.

'You're crying.'

There was curiosity as well as caring in his voice and Selina tensed instinctively. She was still not ready to reveal the truth and probably never would be now. It was enough that she knew herself loved, no matter how remotely.

'Piers thinks we're lovers.' She blurted out the first excuse that sprang to her lips and saw Sir Gerald frown in disbelief.

'It's true,' she cried wildly. 'He thinks I'm some sort of adventuress bent on finding myself a wealthy lover…'

'Most illogical of him,' was Sir Gerald's initial comment. 'Why on earth should he make such a ridiculous assumption… Ridiculous in that a pretty, intelligent young girl like you would even look at an old man like me,' he explained tightly.

'He thinks I'm motivated by money…greed,' Selina explained. She would have said more but the telephone shrilled and Sir Gerald went to answer it.

By the time he had finished Selina had had time to collect herself, her expression calm and slightly wary. 'I think I'll go for a walk before dinner,' she told him lightly.

He didn't argue, but simply looked rather intently at her. 'Yes…' he said at last, 'but don't go too far. They're forecasting thunder and it's been very oppressive all day. There's a very pleasant walk along the river bank which I always find particularly soothing when I've got something on my mind. Something to do with the movement of the water, I suspect.'

Giving him a brief smile, Selina opened the door.

She didn't see anyone as she headed for the river bank, for which she was extremely thankful. Still intensely keyed up from Piers' lovemaking and harsh rejection, it was hard for her to absorb all that Sir Gerald had told her. He had been scrupulous in avoiding laying all the blame for their affair on her mother's shoulders and for that alone she would have loved him, but his evident concern and anguish over the child he had fathered, so different from the emotions she had thought her conception had aroused within him for so many years, were something she was finding it hard to come to terms with. There was pleasure in the knowledge of course, but there was also pain and anguish...sorrow too in having to acknowledge that there was no other decision he could have made in the circumstances. An adult's perception of life differed vastly from a child's and having met Mary she could well understand that he would have been loathe to cause her additional pain and humiliation.

But it was what her father had revealed to her about Piers that occupied most of her thoughts. Now she could recognise that what she had thought of as contempt of her sex was in reality mistrust; carefully camouflaged it was true, but mistrust none the less. Her heart ached for the confused, hurt pre-teenager he must have been. She could well understand how he had fallen under her mother's spell. Selina had watched her charm the opposite sex too often to doubt her success in that sphere. Poor little boy, he hadn't really stood a chance and of course her mother had simply been using him; as she had in effect used her. Once Piers had betrayed her, no matter how innocently, she would have turned on him like all the Furies.

Selina stopped abruptly, staring unseeingly across the calm, slow moving water of the river, unaware of the heavy tension in the atmosphere presaging thunder. Any foolish faint hopes she might have cherished that Piers might return her love must surely now die. How could he love the daughter of the woman who had caused him so much pain?

I must get away from here, Selina thought feverishly. She must escape before it was too late and she was no longer capable of removing herself from his life. He still desired her. She was woman enough to recognise that, but if he learned who she was he would surely resent that desire even more than he already did.

The path running alongside the river petered out abruptly. Deeply lost in her own thoughts Selina hadn't realised how far she had come. The evening sky had taken on a brassy, ominous glow, the atmosphere heavy with the threat of rain, but she wasn't ready to go back yet. The path ahead was blocked by brambles and nettles, but another path led away from the river bank, she could see a stile and fields beyond. Automatically she walked along it. Once over the stile the field stretched out ahead of her, dull gold and stubbly where the farmer had taken an early crop.

There were several large landowners in the area, Mary had told her. Most of the small farms had long since been swallowed up by larger ones and here and there on the rolling hillside in front of her she could see the crumbling remains of these old farmhouses. Too rural as yet to have been caught up in the property development boom these buildings had been left to rot when the land that went with them was acquired by larger landowners.

Dorset was a pretty county, Selina acknowledged, in many aspects still truly rural. This evening in the heavy stillness of the calm before the storm that had threatened all day she felt as though she had the entire countryside to herself. Unwilling to go back, even though she knew she should, she plodded steadily on, pausing now and again to admire the view or to study the wild flowers growing in the ditch alongside the path.

It was only when thunder rolled ominously

closer than she had expected that she realised how far she had come. A glance at her watch confirmed that she had been walking for close on two hours. Storm clouds rolled in quickly even as she stood debating what to do, lightning zig-zagging across the pewter sky.

Knowing that the only sensible thing to do was to turn back, she was just doing so when she felt the first spots of rain. Within seconds, or so it seemed, she was soaked by the intensity of the heavy cloudburst. Thunder crashed mightily overhead, lightning darting frighteningly from the dark clouds.

Stories she had read of people being struck down and killed by just such heavy summer storms flickered in and out of her mind, increasing her pace until she was almost running, her heart thudding madly. The thin cotton skirt and blouse she had come out in were plastered to her skin, her hair hanging in rats tails, her thin sandals soaked through and rubbing against her feet. Head down she stumbled and slid along the now slippery path, the breath almost knocked out of her as she ran into something hard and unyielding. The shock of the unexpected contact made her cry out, the sound silenced as hands gripped her arms and she heard Piers' voice grating in her ear. 'You damned fool… Why the hell didn't you turn back sooner… You're soaked through.'

She wasn't the only one, she realised when she had recovered from her shock. Despite the protection of the oilskin he had pulled on, Piers' hair was plastered darkly to his skull, his jeans a dense dark blue beneath the hem of the oilskin where they had soaked up the rain.

Why had he come after her? Shivering slightly as the damp penetrated through her outer layer of clothes and touched clammy fingers to her skin Selina told herself sardonically that his actions would not have been motivated by any tender emotions. No doubt he thought that left to her own devices she was perfectly capable of seducing any poor unfortunate farm worker she might have come across and had therefore seen it as his duty to protect the same from her. The thought brought a faint smile to her lips and as he turned and saw it, Piers' eyebrows lifted queryingly, his 'What the devil's so amusing,' almost blown away by the fierce crack of thunder sounding nearly overhead.

'Come on, this way…' He grabbed her hand without waiting for her reply, tugging her, not back down the path, but across the field, where the stubble chaffed her bare ankles like sharp needles and she was left gasping too much for breath to question where he was taking her. The field sloped quite steeply upwards and as they reached the crest of it Selina saw in the dip below a sturdy looking stone-built barn, and guessed that Piers intended them to shelter there until the worst of the storm was over.

She didn't really see the point. They were already both so wet that an additional soaking could hardly make much difference, but even as she framed the thought thunder clashed titanically over to her right, jagged darts of lightning illuminating the by now almost dark landscape. 'That's better. At least we're out of the way of those damned trees.'

Although she was out of breath, Piers was barely panting. Turning to look back in the direction he was facing Selina realised that the pathway along which she had come was lined on one side with a good many gnarled and ancient oaks, and she shivered a little as much from the thought of what could have happened had they been standing under one should lightning have struck, as from the cold and damp. Even as she watched the sky was split by fierce white light. A cracking sound that had nothing to do with the thunder riveted her eyes to the smouldering trunk of one of the oaks, a heavy branch thudding across the path they had been on, as the lightning found its target.

'Let's get inside the barn.' Piers had to shout to make himself heard above the storm, and Selina followed him gladly, still shivering with reaction from what she had seen.

The heavy wooden doors were barred with a stout plank thrust through iron supports, but Piers quickly pulled it free, beckoning her inside, and then pulling the door closed behind him, instantly muffling the furious sound of the storm.

The barn smelled of hay and heat, only one small window allowing in a shaft of sullen light.

Selina studied her surroundings tensely, avoiding glancing in Piers' direction. He was busy securing the door of the barn by propping the plank up against it and wedging it closed. The atmosphere inside was almost suffocating, Selina thought nervously; the heat given off by the hay making it hard for her to breathe, or was it Piers' presence and the sense of being cut off from the rest of human life by the ferocity of the storm that was causing her sense of breathlessness?

'What the hell possessed you? You must have seen what was coming. Why didn't you turn back?'

She could feel the violence emanating from him and had a childish desire to burst into tears. Instead she snapped crossly, 'I didn't ask you to come after me… I was on my way back, I would have been perfectly all right.'

'Yeah, sure, if you managed to avoid being struck by lightning. You saw what happened to that tree out there. You could have been underneath it, you do realise that don't you? That path is lined with the damn things… You might have been killed.'

'Much you'd care,' Selina muttered under her breath, stunned when she felt his fingers digging into her arms, whirling her round to face him, his skin drawn back tautly against his bones, his eyes, even in the half-light, blazingly angry as they stared into hers.

'We're not children playing games, Selina,' he

threw at her bitterly. 'We're both adults, or supposed to be… Gerald spoke to me…' he added. 'It seems I owe you one apology at least…'

'Because Sir Gerald told you we weren't lovers?' Her chin tilted, pain mingling with the bitterness she could feel welling up inside her. 'Sorry but an apology based on what someone else tells you isn't acceptable… I'd have preferred you to believe *me*.'

She saw him change colour and wished she hadn't spoken so hastily when she saw the bitterness changing the colour of his eyes from blue to dark navy.

'What is it you want from me?' he demanded thickly, 'Blood?'

What would he say if she replied 'No, love.' Almost she broke into hysterical laughter at the thought of his contempt. Suddenly she started to shiver violently. Piers made a sound under his breath and said tersely, 'Get those wet things off. There's no saying how long we'll have to stay here…it could be hours. I know these summer storms. This part of the world is notorious for them… Something to do with the formation of the hills round here…'

'Won't they worry when we don't get back?' Her throat had gone stiff with panic, and she said the first thing that came into her head—anything to dispel the creepingly insidious feeling of intimacy filtering into their surroundings.

'Gerald will realise that we've taken shelter somewhere,' Piers responded crisply. 'He, too, knows what these storms are like.'

'We could hardly get any more wet than we already are,' Selina pointed out, loathe to spend any more time alone with him than she needed to do.

'Perhaps not…but we could be under another tree when it's struck by lightning… The storm hasn't gone. We could be struck by it ourselves…'

'So could this barn,' Selina pointed out determinedly, trying to dispel the chilling picture he was drawing.

'Unlikely. It's down in a dip…lightning always strikes at the highest point. We should be relatively safe here.'

'How long do you think we'll have to stay here…' She could feel her tension increasing, her muscles rigidly refusing to relax. She didn't want to be here in this intimately enclosed world, with Piers. She was frightened of the feelings he aroused inside her, knowing the potency of them now as she had not done before. His hair was slicked down to his skull, dripping rain water, and as he shrugged off his protective oilcloth she could see where the rain had seeped through the fastenings, his shirt clinging damply to his skin. She wanted to reach out and touch him so badly she was shivering with the effort of stopping herself. Piers saw her shiver and misread the cause of it, frowning darkly. 'I won't say it again, Selina, get out of those wet things. Pneumonia must be the last thing you want... After me of course,' he added tauntingly, his eyes narrowing as he saw the flush that ran up under her pale skin.

'I...I haven't got anything to put on.' How stupid the protest sounded; such a statement of the obvious that she wasn't surprised to see his mouth curl in derision.

'What are you worried about? That the sight of your underwear-clad body might drive me into an orgy of lust? I do have a modicom of self-control you know. Oh for God's sake.' He swore softly, when she continued to shiver without moving. 'Have some sense woman... You're soaked through. God knows how long we'll be stuck here. You can have my shirt if you're so concerned about preserving your modesty. It isn't completely dry, but it's a damn sight dryer than what you've got on.'

She wanted to protest that she didn't want his shirt, that she didn't want anything of his, but when he stripped it off and tossed it over to her she caught it with hands that trembled, overwhelmed by the heated male scent of him that clung to the soft fabric.

She turned her back on him while she stripped off her soaking skirt and blouse. Her bra and panties were wet too, but she wasn't going to take them off. They were only thin silk and should dry out in the heat of this barn, surely?

Behind her she heard the metallic sound of Piers' zip, and then a brief curse. She looked back automatically flushing as he raised his head to glance coolly at her. 'These damn jeans,' he complained wryly. 'They're so wet I can hardly get them off.'

Selina averted her eyes as he tugged the offending fabric downwards, revealing the hard muscles of his thighs. She remembered how she had touched him and how he had reacted and shuddered tensely, her body suddenly weak and yielding…wanting to touch him…wanting to be stroked and caressed to that mindless state of pleasure he had shown her before.

Turning away from him she pulled on his shirt, rolling up the sleeves to her elbows and fastening the buttons with fingers that suddenly seemed clumsy.

'Well now…' He must have got his jeans off, because he was standing behind her; she could feel his warm breath raising goosebumps on her skin. 'What do you propose we do to pass the time…?'

'I hadn't given it much thought.' How stilted and uncertain her voice sounded, more like that of a nervous adolescent than a woman in her mid-twenties.

'Well we could always play guessing games,' Piers told her silkily. 'You still haven't told me what you were doing in Gerald's desk, have you?'

He saw her expression and laughed cynically. 'Did you honestly think I had forgotten? You may stand acquitted of trying to seduce my uncle away from his wife, but there are other charges still outstanding…'

'I thought in this country, a person was presumed innocent until found guilty,' Selina retorted wildly, hating him for the way he was looking at her…hating herself for not being able to deny his accusations…to fling the truth at him, but how could she? How could she tell him that she was the daughter of the woman who had beguiled and then humiliated him?

'Oh yes, but you, my dear Selina, are very far from being innocent, are you?'

The double entendre held in the soft words infuriated her. How dare he presume to judge her morals…as though…as though he himself was as pure as the driven snow.

Her chin tilted firmly, her eyes flashing a dark challenge.

'These days it's as acceptable for a woman to be sexually experienced as it is a man.'

'Oh indeed, but then there's experience and experience, isn't there, Selina…perhaps we could pass the time recounting to one another how we gained our mutual experience?'

His cool mockery stung; his sexual sophistication something that she could not possibly match.

'I think I'd prefer to get some sleep,' she told

him curtly. 'I'm feeling rather tired...and hungry...and since you say we might be here some time it seems like the best thing to do... And certainly more enjoyable than...'

'My company?' he supplied for her, a tight white line round his mouth that belied his apparent calmness. 'By all means go to sleep. In fact I think I might join you. I'm still suffering from the after effects of jet lag, I suspect.'

He did look tired, Selina acknowledged, looking covertly at him as he picked up the oilskin and spread it damp side down on a convenient pile of hay. She didn't want to lie down beside him, Selina thought numbly watching him at his task. Lean and tanned, she could see the muscled play of his body as he worked. Clad only in a pair of dark briefs he looked as urbane as though he were dressed in a Savile Row suit. Her stomach muscles clenched as she watched him, the desire to reach out and touch him almost overpoweringly intense. Quickly she turned away, only to start as he came up behind her and murmured, 'Madam's couch awaits...'

What could she do? To refuse to share the make-shift bed with him would only result in a spate of questions she was ill-equipped to answer. If he should get just one inkling of the truth he would pounce on it and not stop until he dragged every humiliating ounce of satisfaction from it. No, she could not refuse, Selina acknowledged, shivering a little as she walked unsteadily over to where he had spread the oilskin.

Despite its earlier heat the temperature in the barn was dropping rapidly. Outside the rain lashed down, driven now by a fierce, buffeting wind.

Overhead the thunder still rolled, spasmodic flashes of lightning illuminating the heavy darkness that had fallen.

'How long will we have to stay here?' She couldn't prevent herself from asking the craven question. Piers frowned and glanced towards the small window.

'It's hard to say…until the storm dies out…it would be stupid to attempt the walk back until then. It's at least four miles… What on earth possessed you to set out on such a marathon? Gerald warned you there was a storm in the offing…'

'I was thinking,' Selina told him, biting her lip when she saw the way he was looking at her.

'Very deep thoughts, too, to judge from the

distance you walked. Very deep indeed if they prevented you from seeing what should have been obvious to even the most town-bred fool.'

'I didn't ask you to come after me,' Selina retorted spiritedly. He didn't need to keep reminding her that she had acted thoughtlessly.

'No...'

She half-expected him to say that Gerald had sent him after her, but instead he said nothing, still simply looking at her. 'I realise how little you want my company,' he said harshly at last, 'but to attempt to walk back now in this rain and darkness is asking for trouble. The path will be a mud-stream by now... One or both of us could easily slip and sprain an ankle... Why put ourselves to such a stupid risk when we can stay here in comparative warmth and complete safety?'

'I'm hungry.' Selina knew she was being childish, but she couldn't help it. It stopped her from reacting too much to his presence.

He walked over to the oilskin and flipped it back, reaching into one of the pockets. A rare grin lightened his expression as he produced a bar of chocolate. 'Here you are, little girl,' he mocked indulgently. 'Eat that...'

He threw it over to her, and Selina caught it clumsily, suddenly feeling guilty because she was being so churlish. He wasn't to know that her reaction sprang from her intense fear that he might realise how she felt about him.

The chocolate felt soft inside its silver wrapper, and when she broke it in half, chocolate clung stickily to her fingers. Tentatively she held out one half to him and said shakily, 'Want to go shares?'

His smile rocked her back on her heels. It changed his entire expression, and she felt ridiculously eager to respond to it, to bask in its warmth. 'I thought you'd never ask.' He took it from her with one hand, grasping her wrist with the other. His tongue was rough and deliciously sensual as he licked the chocolate off her fingers; shock waves of pleasure storming through her body as she tried not to react to the unexpected contact. Her fingers closed together, curling up in protest, but he caught them in his mouth, sucking them slowly as though savouring the lingering taste of the chocolate. When he eventually released her Selina could find no words to break the heavy silence, but Piers did it for her.

'It *was* part of my half,' he told her judiciously,

and in the sudden darkness, eclipsing the faint light in the room as heavy clouds rolled up obscuring the faint moon, Selina could not tell whether the smile she sensed in his voice was actually mirrored on his lips.

She ate her chocolate without tasting it, her stomach churning wildly as she re-lived the touch of his tongue against her skin. Her body was burning with a fierce primaeval heat; aching with a need she didn't want to admit to.

When he said teasingly, 'Come on, bedtime for little girls,' she walked blindly without a word over to the oilskin, obeying him as though she had been programmed to do so.

She would never sleep, she thought achingly, lying down carefully so that she wasn't taking up more than half of the make-shift bed, turning to face outwards, careful not to let her body come into contact with Piers' in any way as he lay down beside her.

The darkness was almost stygian now; a sign that the storm was far from abating. 'There's something extraordinarily satisfying about being warm, dry and safe, while the storm rages all around one, don't you think?'

The sound of Piers' voice, light and yet threaded with an unfamiliar tension, surprised her. As though he sensed her feelings he said quietly, 'I know there is still a good deal between us that has to be resolved Selina. I know I was mistaken about you where Gerald is concerned... I also know you're still hiding something from me, but for tonight at least could we not call a truce?'

What game was he playing with her now? Was he trying to lull her into a false sense of security before turning on her again? But if she refused would he simply not press her all the harder; determined to find out the truth?

'Truce,' she said slowly, knowing there was really nothing else she could say.

Surely that wasn't relief she heard in his voice as he added softly, 'You know if our positions were reversed, being the gentleman that I am I should feel obliged if not to share my borrowed shirt with you then at least to share a little of my body heat. I'm cold,' he complained. 'Come a bit closer to me, there's a good girl. That way we can both keep warm.'

What he was saying made sense, but every

instinct she possessed shrieked a rejection of
what he was suggesting. She didn't want to be
close to him... She didn't know if she could
handle the strain it would put on her already
over-loaded nervous system, but it seemed she
had little choice, Piers was already moving close
behind her, his arm curling round her waist and
pulling her back against his body, his breath
warm and even against her skin.

His muffled 'That's better,' grazed the
delicate nerve endings of her ear, pleasure shivering through her. 'See,' he added softly.
'You're cold too.'

Cold? Selina repressed a desire to laugh hys-
terically. Her body was overheating madly, overheating and over-reacting. There was nothing
she wanted to do more than to turn in his arms,
and press herself the length of him; breast to
beast, thigh to thigh; absorbing the heat and
maleness of him...

His hand rested impersonally on her waist,
bringing her back to reality. For Piers their close-
ness was simply a matter of necessity; of prac-
ticality. Silently Selina prayed for a miracle—an
ending of the storm and enough light for them

to make the walk back, but a glance at her watch shocked her as she realised the time. It was gone ten in the evening. There would be no light tonight, so she might just as well resign herself to their situation. She closed her eyes, trying to relax her body into sleep but too tensely aware of Piers lying against her back to do more than monitor his steady breathing while she tried to match her own to it.

CHAPTER NINE

SHE must have slept. She realised that the moment she opened her eyes, her body cramped and stiff as she tried to turn over and realised too late where she was and with whom. Piers was still lying curled against her back, and as she tried to move he muttered a thick protest deep in his throat, his arm tightening around her.

Even while she was apprehensive, tremors of pleasure rippled through her body, to the extent of lulling her with idyllic daydreams that she and Piers were established lovers; that he returned her feelings and that any moment now he would open his eyes and gaze into hers with warmth and love.

Idiot, she chided herself, trying to wriggle away without disturbing him. Nothing could be less romantic than the aggravating prickle of straw beneath Piers' protective oilskin, and she ought to know by now that the last emotion she would ever see in Piers' eyes would be the one she longed so much to see.

'Stop wriggling.'

The sleepy command tensed her into shocked awareness of the fact that he *was* awake. It was still pitch dark, impossible for him to read the truth in her eyes, even if she had been lying facing him, which she wasn't. He was only another human being, she told herself sardonically. He had no special powers that made it possible for him to read her mind.

Now that he was awake she expected him to remove his arm and turn away from her, but instead it tightened still further, drawing her back into the warmth of his body.

'Umm, that's better.'

'Let me go.' Her protest was fierce and slightly husky, his answering laughter grazing the back of her neck and the vulnerable skin behind her ear, making her shiver visibly.

'What and lose my human hot-water bottle?' His hand moved slightly, settling against her midriff, his fingers against her heart, monitoring its rapid thud. 'You're as tense as a virgin sharing a bed with a man for the first time,' he commented lazily. 'We both know it can't possibly be fear of my sex that's causing your tension, so what is it? Fear of me? Fear that you might in a moment of weakness betray the truth to me?'

Even now he wasn't prepared to relax his suspicion of her. Pain flared burningly to life inside her, making her lash out wildly at him. 'You're so caught up in your self-appointed task of proving the entire female sex untrustworthy that you aren't capable of recognising the truth.'

His fingers against her heart tensed painfully and Selina found she was holding her breath. The grip he used to turn her round to face him wasn't a tender one, and even though the darkness made it impossible for her to see his face clearly she could feel the tension emanating from him.

'And just what makes you say that?'

His voice was like steel, incisive and hard, willing her to take back her impulsive words, but she refused to be dominated by his court-room icyness. Having come so far she was, suddenly, not prepared to cede victory to him. Pride and a burst of temper carried her into angry speech.

'Sir Gerald told me how the…the woman he was involved with hurt you. I think you've been punishing my sex for that ever since.'

The silence was dreadful; a chasm that stretched unbridgeable between them; its depths armed with sharp knives ready to destroy the unwary. Now Selina was glad of the darkness, and although one half of her regretted what she had said, the other rejoiced in her strength in being able to do so. For too long she had cowered under the pressure of Piers' disapproval and contempt; neither of which she had done anything to earn… Not if one discounted the fact that she was her mother's daughter, but that was something she refused to think of now. It would weaken her too much.

'Quite the amateur psychologist aren't we?' Piers said bitingly at last. 'I wonder what made my uncle give you that piece of information?'

Selina wasn't prepared to tell him.

'Unfortunately, the conclusions you have drawn from it are wildly incorrect. If I mistrust certain members of your sex it is because my legal training suggests that I have grounds for doing so. In your own case I would say that those grounds are extremely strong. I still haven't had an explanation of what you were doing with my uncle's papers. I still believe there is something you are hiding from me.'

Selina was beginning to wish she had never brought the subject up. As always, Piers had turned it to his own advantage and she was fast losing the initial ground she had gained. She moved restlessly, suddenly aware of the pressure of his fingers digging into her arms.

'The thunder's stopped,' she said huskily. 'Why don't we start back?'

'It's three in the morning…the house will be locked up, and we'll only disturb everyone.'

'But surely they'll be worrying about us?'

'I doubt it. Gerald will guess that we've taken refuge somewhere. What's the matter, Selina? Scared of being alone here with me?'

The conversation had come full circle.

'Why should I be?' She attempted a brief shrug and winced under the pressure of his grip.

'Oh, I could think of several excellent reasons.' His voice was soft, dangerously so, and she felt the coolness of his breath grazing her cheek as he bent his head towards her, 'Including this one.'

If his kiss had been punishing, contemptuous, as she had expected it would be, she might have stood some chance of withstanding it, but instead the movement of his mouth against her own was no more than the lightest whisper, encouraging her lips to soften and part in bewildered pleasure.

He raised his head and studied her in the darkness, although what he could see of her features she wasn't sure. Enough, it seemed to reach out and trace the shape of her mouth with cool fingers until she shivered in mute acknowledgment of the feelings he aroused within her.

She knew she could have stopped him with a word, but that word refused to be spoken, instead she stared in silence as he pulled her into the warmth of his body, securing her there with one hand, while the thumb of the other probed the pulse thudding furiously on the inside of her wrist. When he lifted it to his mouth stroking it with his tongue, firebolts of desire seemed to be unleashed inside her, turning her weak and yielding, on fire with the hunger his touch aroused. His tongue caressed her palm, making her shiver hectically and cling to him, fiercely glad that he wasn't wearing his shirt. His skin felt hot beneath her hands, or was it from her own hands which she was running feverishly over the solid muscles of his chest, that the heat was coming?

She moaned deep in her throat when he took her fingers into his mouth, sucking them slowly, consumed by waves of desire as intense as sheet lightning. He was melting her bones with pleasure, turning her into a fluid, pliable formless being that he could mould to his own desire.

The rough abrasion of his thigh against her own seared her with heat, her fingers digging into the muscles of his back as he released her fingers to nibble delicate kisses along her throat. It seemed he was only playing with her, fuelling her need for him with light, almost teasing kisses and caresses, but there was nothing light or teasing about the aroused pressure of his lower body, pressing hers down into the oilskin, totally male and demanding in the message it was communicating to her.

He cupped and stroked her breasts, and although she tried to conceal from him the frenzy his touch was driving her to, a small moan forced its way past her closed lips.

'Do you want me?'

How could he imagine otherwise? Pride warned her that she would be wise to deny it; he could simply be arousing her for the pleasure of making her ache and leaving her unsatisfied, but some deep and intensely feminine core of her refused to allow her to resort to any subterfuge. Her hands on his shoulders she sought out the darkly shadowed outline of his face, fixing her eyes on the gleaming darkness of his.

'Yes, I do,' she said simply, and in saying it she felt as though she had committed herself to the tidal flood of waters far too deep for her to swim unsupported in. Although he didn't realise it, by her admission she had placed in him a trust he would never give to her. Not knowing what his reaction would be, she waited tensely, already preparing herself mentally and physically for his rejection.

She felt him exhale as though the breath had been tensely contained, his chest compressing. 'Dear God, then show me that you do,' he muttered hoarsely, the ragged, almost tortured sound of his voice stunning her.

'I've been through hell, wanting you, do you know that?' The raw admission held her

immobile, only his thick, almost guttural exclamation of despair, driving her to react instinctively and enclose his body with her arms, her
lips pressing tender, reassuring kisses against his
throat as she tried to come to terms with the
mental anguish in his voice. It hurt her to think
of him in pain. Not for a minute did she stop to
think that this might be another ploy; another
method of undermining her defences, her every
instinct to stem his pain.

His hands gripped her waist tightly, his throat
tipping back under the light pressure of her
mouth. Her kisses had been instinctive, designed
to comfort and reassure, but as she looked down
at him Selina could sense the sexual hunger he
was barely able to control and as though her
body was acutely attuned to the needs of his she
shivered in response to it, lowering her head to
touch her mouth at first tentatively, and then
more surely to the masculine line of his throat.

His uninhibited response to her touch surprised
her. He was normally so controlled and contained
she had thought that somehow he would control his
sexual desire in the same way that he controlled the
other aspects of his life. Instead he moaned her

name with hoarse need, his fingers burrowing into her hair as he held her against him, her mouth tremulous as it touched the rigid muscles of his throat and felt him tremble against her.

Lost in the pleasure of discovering how much she could arouse him, it came as a shock to find herself suddenly thrust away from his body and rolled underneath him, the weight of his torso pinning her down, his palms cupping her jaw, holding her so that it would have been impossible for her to evade the bruising passion of his kiss even if she had wanted to.

His mouth moved urgently on hers, compelling an equally urgent response. The barrier of his shirt and their underclothes was a physical agony it almost hurt to endure. As though the same thought had struck him, Piers removed his hands from her face, lifting her body slightly without breaking the kiss. She moved willingly with him, making a small sound of satisfaction deep in her throat when he unfastened her bra. The slow slide of his fingers against her skin removing both his borrowed shirt and her bra was almost torture. When she was finally free to arch her body into the heat of his she shuddered deeply.

Piers broke the kiss to mutter throatily. 'Night after night I've dreamed of you like this. Melting in my arms, on fire for me…wanting me as you've never wanted any of your other lovers…'

It should have put a brake on her need for him, but it didn't. Nothing, but nothing, was more important than this aching, crazy hunger his touch stroked up inside her, and she responded feverishly to every touch of his hands against her body, scattering wild kisses against his shoulders and neck, interspersing them with small female sounds of pleasure when his hands found her breasts, shaping and caressing them until she was writhing wantonly against him, her body shameless in its invitation to his.

Piers released her and she shivered in the sudden access of cold air, desperately straining her eyes to make out the male shape of his body as he moved away from her. What was happening? Had he simply been playing a game with her? But no…surely no one could fake the desire she had read in his kisses; felt in his body.

He moved again, the faint light filtering into the room revealing the aroused, tormented expression on his face. Pity and love welled up inside her… He wanted her and yet at the same time he hated himself for doing so. She knew that as clearly as though she had heard him say the words. This was the time for her to pull back…to make the decision for both of them.

Kneeling beside her Piers cupped her breast, slowly anointing it with his mouth—the lightest most delicate touch; and yet enough to banish forever any thought of stopping him from what he was doing. Her other breast was revered in the same fashion; the ache of wanting his complete possession churning hotly through her stomach. She reached out to touch him and encountered the muscled hardness of his thigh. Her fingers stirred the roughly male hairs. She felt him tense and shudder; his mouth, which had been caressing the valley between her breasts, suddenly hot and demanding, his voice hoarse and ragged as he raised his head and muttered in her ear. 'Dear God, do you know how much I've wanted you to touch me like that?'

He took her hand, placing it against the hard, throbbing swell of his manhood, his mouth covering hers, deeply; hungrily; moving over its softness in increasing fierce demand as she traced the rigid flesh beneath her fingers, exploratively at first and then caressingly as she heard the moaned sounds of pleasure stifled in his throat, his tongue hot and possessive as he explored the inner sweetness of her mouth.

Beneath her hand his body pulsed and shuddered, his mouth wild and hot as he caressed her throat and then moved lower down to her breasts, making her shudder as convulsively as he was doing himself as his tongue stroked roughly over her taut nipples and his teeth bit delicately into her tender flesh. Her body arched and moved seductively, instinct taking over from logic. She wanted him with an intensity she had never imagined herself feeling for any man, Selina realised shakily. She wanted him with a primitive urgency that made her wonder at her own loss of self-control. Her hand moved yearningly against his body, communicating her need. Piers moaned deep in his throat, muttering her name thickly, pressing himself against her in a mute demand for her continued caress.

'Dear God, you're driving me almost insane. Do you know that?' The words were ragged and tortured, moaned against her mouth before it was covered by his. Selina tried to move closer to him, wanting the hard male pressure of him against her lower body, but he gripped her wrist, keeping her hand where it was, his voice thick and slurred as he muttered. 'No… no…not yet. I want to know all of you…' he added hoarsely. 'I want to touch and taste every inch of you.'

His hands moved over her body, and when they came to the barrier of her briefs Selina trembled in need and tension. He tugged her panties down, his fingers closing round her ankle, caressing the fine bones until she shivered, her hands sliding up his body to grasp his shoulders as she felt the warm pressure of his mouth against her skin, teasing a delicate line of kisses over her calf, behind her knee, along the inside of her thigh. Her breath seemed to be trapped in her throat, her heart pounding erratically. His fingers touched her intimately, unleashing a wild flood of pleasure. She wanted to draw back away from the intimacy and yet she wanted also to prolong it, to respond wantonly to the delicate pressure of his touch.

'What's wrong?' His voice was tense, almost curt. 'Don't you like what I'm doing? Tell me what you do like… You're a woman of experience who knows what turns her on.'

Waves of shock coursed through her. She wanted to deny his assertion, to blurt out the truth, but some deep-seated instinct warned her that if she did so, he would withdraw from her. She was a virgin, and if he knew that he would probably stop making love to her, and then she would have nothing…nothing at all to hold to her during the long, lonely nights that lay ahead.

'Fool, he's going to find out anyway,' an inner voice taunted, but by then it would be too late…her own duplicity shocked her. Was this what loving him had brought her to?

His fingers stroked and caressed, her mind unable to control her body's almost delirious response. She shuddered and writhed, abandoning herself completely to the feelings he was arousing; deep, intense feelings carrying her along with them like a fast-flowing river, taking her to a culmination that she sensed dimly, but could not entirely envisage. Her hands had been clenched into Piers' shoulders, but under the rhythmic stroke of his fingers she found them sliding downwards, her fingers stroking along the dark arrowing of hair that led past his navel, lower, and lower until she was enclosing him with tremulous fingers, feeling the life pulse beating up under his flesh.

They had been lying side by side, facing one another, but now, suddenly Piers disengaged himself from her, sitting up, pulling her towards and across his body so that her head lay in his lap, her body curled towards him.

His fingers trembled as he brushed her hair away from her face, his voice thick and uneven as he muttered, 'I can't stand much more of this... Are you enjoying tormenting me, is that what it is?' She wasn't sure what he meant and was even less sure when he added rawly, 'Perhaps I ought to indulge in a little torment of my own.'

His fingers found her again, inciting a slow, languorous pleasure that built quickly into the same pulsating need she had felt before. She moaned wildly, her body arching, her mouth hot and tremulous as she pressed it into the hard flesh of his thigh to stop herself from begging him for release. Her body was shivering violently, pulsing with a need she had not known existed, driven on by desires and hungers outside her control. She felt the heat of Piers' mouth sear her inner thigh and cried out in protest, anxiously trying to move away from him, her mind shocked by the intimacy of his caress, even while her body apparently craved it. Without being aware of it she had curled her fingers tightly into his thigh, and when he bit delicately into her skin she released them in sudden shock, his voice almost unrecognisable as he demanded hoarsely, 'Touch me Selina…kiss me…'

She knew suddenly what he wanted and while her mind struggled to come to terms with the intimacy of his desire, her own body started to melt beneath the delicate stroke of his tongue, caressing her until she was mindless with the pleasure of it, trying to pull away from him with one breath only to give in to the waves of sensual pleasure exploding inside her with the next. Without conscious thought she reacted instinctively, searching out his maleness, stroking and caressing its pulsating power, her mouth hot and tremulous against his skin, her shyness and uncertainty banished by his hoarse sounds of pleasure, by the fever he was arousing within her by his touch.

When he suddenly pulled away from her, her sense of deprivation was acutely shocking. She tensed in fear and rejection, not knowing what she had done wrong, terrified that he had somehow realised the truth and meant to tell her so, all her earlier fears that he was simply playing a part, returning to torment her.

In the dim light she could just make out the outline of his face, and what she saw there both reassured and scared her. He still wanted her…that much she could see, but suddenly she was very much aware of her own inexperience; of the ache deep within her body; of the flooding waves of pleasure his touch had engendered, of her own new knowledge of what it meant to arouse a man, to touch and caress him until his desire was at the fever pitch she could see flaming in Piers' eyes.

'Afterwards he'll hate you for deceiving him,' a small voice warned, but wantonly she ignored it, watching him staring down at her as though waiting for some signal.

Her body trembled and she looked back at him in mute entreaty, her voice thready and uncertain as she begged, 'Piers…please make love to me.'

The weight and heat of his body against hers made her shudder with pleasure. It felt so good to have the warm satin of his skin caressing her own, his thigh between hers, hard and firm, stilling the wild trembling in her body. He moved, arching over her, his mouth, hot and hungry on hers, whirling away her fears. Her body lifted to meet the fierce thrust of his, absorbing the brief shock wave of pain. She thought she felt Piers tense and she moved urgently against him, her fingers curling into his back, her gasp of mingled pain and pleasure as he thrust deeper into her lost beneath the heat of his mouth.

Waves of pleasure built up inside her, finally exploding cataclysmically, her sharp, shuddering gasps of fulfilment echoed by the harsh male sounds Piers compressed against her skin.

Filled with the wonder of what had happened, she was dimly aware of Piers harsh breathing gradually slowing down; his heart hammering heavily against her ribs. His fingers gripped her wrist, his harsh exclamation of her name forcing her to look at him and realise that it wasn't exhaustion that made his heart hammer, but anger.

'Why?' He lifted his weight away from her as he asked the question, shaking her slightly as he repeated it, 'Why?'

'Why what?' She was tempted to defy him, to pretend she had no idea what he was talking about. Perhaps then he would think he had been wrong, but she had forgotten how hard a man he was to deceive.

'Why didn't you tell me you were a virgin?' he demanded curtly. 'Why did you let me believe you were experienced?'

What could she say? Because she wanted him to make love to her and knew that if he knew the truth he would not? If she said that how long would it be before he guessed the rest? That she had fallen deeply in love with him?

'I didn't think it was important.' She managed to sound carelessly unconcerned, but only by averting her eyes from his. He soon put a stop to this ploy by releasing her wrist to cup her face.

'If it wasn't important, how come I've been your first lover? You're an extremely beautiful woman, Selina…and I can't believe I've been the first man to desire you.'

'Maybe not, but perhaps you're the first I've

desired back in return.' She said it lightly, praying that he wouldn't guess just what her calm words masked. When he was silent, she added tensely, 'I'm tired Piers…surely it isn't that important. We made love because it was what we both wanted. *I* enjoyed it, and I refuse to spoil it by conducting a post-mortem on it.'

She could see his mouth thin and tighten, and arched her eyebrows slightly, 'Logically I'm the one who should play the injured party role, Piers, not you.'

'You knew the truth, I didn't.' He said it flatly, almost accusing her.

'I can't see what difference it makes whether I was a virgin or not.'

'Can't you? Then you're exceptionally naive.' His voice was dry and mocking, and Selina shivered, cold now that she was deprived of the warmth of his body.

'Now isn't the time to discuss it. We'll talk later,' he added curtly, stretching over her to hand her his shirt. 'Put this on, you're cold.'

When her fingers tensed over the buttons he fastened them for her. Tears stung her eyes. She badly wanted some show of tenderness from him right now, but tenderness was the very last thing he was likely to show her. As he moved away from her she could see the outline of his body, lean and very masculine and she shivered, remembering how she had caressed him...how he had wanted her to caress him. Almost as though he read her mind, he said, 'I'll say one thing for you, you're certainly a quick study. If I hadn't had proof positive, I'd never have believed you to be inexperienced.' He had his back to her which probably accounted for the raw, almost angry sound of it. He turned back to her, his mouth still tight. 'You do realise how badly I might have hurt you?'

When she made no response he gripped hold of her, and demanded almost savagely, 'Did I? Did I hurt you?'

More concern, where she wanted love was demeaning and painful. Pride came to her rescue, allowing her to say coolly, 'Did you want to? Is that how you take revenge on my sex?'

He released her, swearing under his breath, pushing angry fingers through his already ruffled hair. 'We can't talk about this now...but talk about it we will, Selina, I promise you that.'

Holding her eyes he said softly, 'You do realise you could have my child?'

She had, but only in the last few seconds, and his awareness of her vulnerability made her lash out and demand sarcastically, 'And if I should be pregnant, what would it mean? That you would have to do the honourable thing and marry me?'

She had meant the words to be a reminder to herself of how little their lovemaking meant to her, but was shocked into silence when he said quietly,

'That's right. There's already been one child born into our family who hasn't known her father. I won't see that happen to another.'

He was talking about *her*, Selina realised numbly....*she* was that child, but hard on the heels of this thought came tearing pain. How could she allow him to marry her, knowing that he despised rather than loved her? No...at all costs she could not allow that to happen. Too tired and exhausted to risk a verbal battle with him that she knew she could only lose, she kept silent, sinking down on to the floor, and turning her back to him. Her actions seemed to irritate him.

'I hardly think either of us is likely to sleep

now,' he told her crisply, 'and that being the case we might as well start back. With a bit of luck by the time we get there someone should be up.'

CHAPTER TEN

IT was almost fully dawn, the sky serene and pale blue, when they finally reached the house. As they walked in silence through the wet garden, a solution suddenly came to Selina. Her mouth went dry with the enormity of it, but she knew shudderingly that it would work; that if she used it there would be no further question of Piers marrying her—child or no child. Although he didn't realise it, it was a measure of her love for him that she was prepared to use it. She loved him too much to trap him in a marriage he had never really wanted. And if she was to have his child? Memories of her own fatherless childhood beat down on her, and yet the thought of aborting Piers' baby was unthinkable…

She would worry about it if and when it happened. What was important now was ensuring that Piers cut her out of his life and permanently. And she knew just the thing.

Mary let them in, her expression concerned when she saw their still damp clothes. 'Thank goodness you're all right. Gerald said that you would be, but I was so concerned.'

'We got caught right in the middle of the thunderstorm,' Piers told his aunt, 'and we decided it was best to take shelter where we could. Luckily we were right by Thompson's winter barn. Hence the straw,' he added with a faint grimace, plucking a couple of stalks from Selina's hair.

'Well let me make both of you a cup of tea. Selina looks exhausted,' Mary commented with renewed concern. 'I'm terrified of thunder, I'm afraid,' she told her commiseratingly. 'Poor Gerald didn't get much sleep last night because I was so restless, so if you feel like spending a lazy morning in bed, I'm sure he won't mind.'

It was a convenient escape route and Selina took it, not daring to look at Piers as she picked up the mug of tea Mary had poured for her.

Piers followed her out of the kitchen, his expression faintly grim. 'We still have to talk,' he warned her. 'You can't run away for ever Selina.'

Not for ever, Selina promised mentally, climbing

the stairs, just for long enough for her to find the courage for what she knew she must do.

Much to her own surprise she fell asleep, waking only when someone opened her bedroom door. Sunlight streamed in through the windows, the sky a soft bright blue, the air wafting through the opening pleasantly fresh now that the storm had cleared the air.

'Don't bother feigning sleep, I know you're awake.'

Her mouth compressed indignantly as she struggled to sit up, thankful that she had taken the time to shower and pull on her cotton night-dress before sliding into bed.

When her bedroom door opened the last person she had expected to see was Piers, and as she controlled the shock waves of pleasure the sight of him brought she realised that he was dressed formally in a dark suit and plain silk shirt.

'I have to leave for the airport in half an hour,' he told her curtly, 'an unexpected complication in New York and they need me back there. I wanted to see you before I left.'

Here it was, her golden opportunity to do what she knew must be done. Sickness crawled through her stomach, her nerves tensing in dread of what was to come.

'When I get back I intend to announce our engagement—we can be married quite quickly.'

'Always supposing there is any need for us to be married,' Selina broke in huskily. Dear God he was offering her heaven and she had to refuse it… She had to both for his sake and her own.

'Whether you are carrying my child or not makes very little difference.' He turned to watch her, his eyes hard and determined as they searched her pale face. 'I was your first lover Selina, which must mean something. You're no adolescent, too young to have experimented with sex. The very fact that you were a virgin tells me that you can't be totally indifferent to me.'

'I wanted you physically, yes.' God how it hurt to make such a statement, but she had to go through with it. 'But that is no basis for a marriage.'

His eyes were burning into hers, an expression twisting his mouth that might almost have been pain if she hadn't known better.

'It's a damned sight more than a good many other couples have.'

'And you'd marry me even with your suspicions about me? You were right to suspect me, Piers.' How cool and controlled she sounded. She almost marvelled at her own ability to act. 'Would you like to know the truth? Very well you shall have it.' Her mouth curled mockingly, her total involvement with the role she knew she had to play so convincingly that he would never suspect what she was doing, bringing a febrile glitter to her eyes, narrowing them to almond slits of anger. 'Yes, I wanted you to make love to me, Piers…and do you know why? Because I wanted to see if you were as vulnerable to me as you were to my mother. Do you know who I am, Piers?' She laughed, wondering if he would guess how much the sound tore at her throat.

His expression hadn't changed; he was standing completely still, only his eyes betraying any trace of emotion. They turned from blue to black, burning into her, making her ache with a need to stop what she was doing, but it was impossible. She was her mother's daughter, and sooner or later Piers would remember that and hate her for it. She would not marry him without him knowing the truth, and he would not marry her once he did. All she was doing was stretch-

ing the truth slightly…stretching it and concealing part of it from him, like the fact that she had
fallen deeply and permanently in love with him,
she told herself wryly.

'Just what the hell are you trying to say?' His
voice was harsh, splintering the fragile silence.
'Stop playing the actress Selina and just tell me…'

'Very well.' Her face cool and unreadable, she
said quietly, 'I am Sir Gerald's illegitimate
daughter; the child of the woman who taught
you to distrust my sex Piers; your cousin…I…'

It was the small explosive sound from the door
that broke the thick silence. It was still open and
Mary stood there, her face drained and pale.
Selina knew with a surge of remorse that she
must have overheard nearly every word.

'Piers, your taxi's here,' she said huskily. 'Shall
I…'

'I'll be right down…' He looked at Selina and
she faced him proudly, as Mary closed the door
and walked away.

'Do you still want to marry me now?' she
asked tauntingly. 'Now that you know the truth
about me?'

'Why did you apply for that job?'

Everything depended on her answer now, Selina sensed. Gripping her hands together beneath the bedclothes, she shrugged coolly and replied. 'Why not? Surely you must agree that my father owes me something...a very substantial something too I should say, especially when one adds on interest for all the years of neglect.'

'You wanted money...revenge...is that it?' He had crossed over to her, his voice harsh as he bent towards her, fierce lights glittering in the darkness of his eyes. 'Haven't you realised yet that in terms of financial worth I'm a far richer man than my uncle? My father was extremely wealthy, and I inherited it all when he died... You've misplayed your card very badly my dear. As my wife you would have had my fortune to run through...and to think I actually...'

'Yes?'

'It doesn't matter.' He walked over to the door and then paused by it, turning to face her. His face was almost grey. It was his pride that was hurt, nothing more, Selina told herself...he didn't love her...that grey tinge to his skin, the way it stretched too tightly over his bones, meant only that his pride was wounded, and she would be a fool if she allowed herself to believe anything else.

'And if you should be carrying my child?'

It was the final hurdle and she took a deep breath to prepare herself for it, forcing a nonchalant shrug, managing to evade his eyes as she said coolly, 'Well I shan't follow my mother's example.'

'You mean you'll have an abortion?' His voice was harsh, tight with something that if she hadn't known him and simply heard it she might have construed as sheer agony.

'What's wrong? Scared that I might ask you to pay for it?'

He slammed the door and came towards her, fury in every line of his body. When he stopped short of the bed she found she was trembling visibly.

'You're not worth giving up several years of my life for,' he told her very softly, 'otherwise, believe me, there's nothing that would give me greater pleasure than to deprive you of another breath.'

He was gone before she could say a word. She heard him clattering down the stairs and then the slam of the front door, followed by the sound of a car drawing away.

It was over. She had done it. She ought to be

feeling relieved, but all she could feel was a vast nothingness…no pain…nothing… But the pain would come later. She knew that. She tried to get out of bed and found that she was trembling so badly she could hardly move. Her bedroom door opened and for a moment she felt a wild surge of hope, but it was Mary who stood there. Remorse coursed through her as she looked at the older woman. She had never meant to hurt her…

'I expect you would like me to leave.' She kept her voice neutral, avoiding the faded hazel eyes.

'Why on earth should I?' Mary crossed the room and sat down on the side of her bed, her eyes wise and very kind. 'My dear, do you know what this will mean to Gerald?'

'He's done his duty by me,' Selina responded shakily, not daring to trust in what she saw in Mary's expression. 'I can only be a reminder of things he'd rather forget.'

'How could he forget the child he had fathered? Indeed if he could he would not have been the man I loved—enough to fight with every weapon I possessed to keep him—even my children. Oh yes,' she said firmly when Selina looked at her. 'I *did* fight for him, and it wasn't an easy fight—or a clean one. I can't tell you the anguish we've both suffered over you. Gerald because he could not give you the attention and love he gave to his other daughters, and myself because I knew that in keeping him I'd deprived you of the right to know your father— a very wonderful and special father, as each one of my daughters would testify.'

'You…you don't hate me?' Selina said it wonderingly, hardly daring to believe what she was hearing.

'Hate *you*? Oh my dear…'

She couldn't remember the last time anyone had touched her with compassion and caring, certainly her mother had never been the type to kiss and cuddle her, and adult though she was she could not stop the tears from forming and rolling down her face as Mary smoothed back her tangled hair and gave her a little shake.

'Foolish, foolish girl,' she chided. 'You should have told us who you were. My dear…this is going to make Gerald so happy. I can't wait to tell him. He's tried so hard over the years to trace you…but he promised your mother he would not interfere in your life. He didn't want you to be torn between two parents who could never be united.'

'I thought he didn't care about me... All my life I've believed that...that he rejected me...'

'Nothing could have been further from the truth. Nor a birthday or Christmas has gone by without him suffering the anguish of losing you.'

'Piers hates me...' She hadn't known she was going to say that until the words were out.

Mary's eyes soft with compassion as she looked at her. 'Piers is a very complex man.'

'Who hated my mother because of what she did to him and to you.'

'But *you* are not your mother Selina,' Mary said quietly. 'Stay here and rest for a while, while I break the good news to G...to your father.' She stood up and smiled down at her, adding softly, 'Don't worry... Believe me, there is nowhere on earth where you'll be more welcome than in this house. It will be marvellous having another daughter about the place. It's selfish of me I know, but I do so miss the girls' company.'

Events were moving with a speed that took Selina's breath away. She had barely come to terms yet with Mary's wholehearted acceptance of her, and now here she was taking it for granted that she would stay here as a member of the family. Part of her longed intensely to do that…to be cosseted and petted by Mary, and yet how could she stay after what she had said to Piers? This was his family too…

Unable to rest or relax she got up and showered, dressing quickly. What would her father say when Mary told him? Perhaps he would not be as ready to accept her as his wife? Her stomach was churning nauseously by the time Mary came back.

'Gerald would like to see you,' was all she said, but the smile she gave her was warm and encouraging.

She found her father sitting in his chair. When she opened the door and glanced uncertainly at him he stood up, holding out his arms to her.

It was several minutes before either of them could speak, and when he did, his words warmed her chilled heart. 'If I could have chosen anyone for my unknown daughter Selina, it would have been you. There has been a bond between us right from the start. Perhaps I should have guessed,' he added with a brief smile. 'All those excellent qualifications…'

'Piers suspected… Well at least he suspected I was concealing something,' she added huskily.

'Yes, he told me. Mary said you were quarrelling this morning. Are you in love with him Selina?'

What could she say? 'Yes,' she admitted shakily, 'but he only desires me…or at least he did, until this morning,' she said wryly. 'Now I think he must hate me. I told him I took the job with you because I wanted money from you…revenge for…for the past, but it wasn't true.'

'My dear, you don't need to tell me that, and if Piers wasn't half-demented with love for you, he'd be able to see that for himself.'

'Piers doesn't love me!'

'No? Then why should such an astute and capable lawyer be so easily deceived with lies that even a first-year trainee could demolish. Selina, I know my nephew.'

PIERS could not love her! It was a thought that was constantly on her mind over the next few days, when the rest of the family had been told the news. Her three half-sisters had reacted so favourably that Selina was overwhelmed by their ready acceptance of her. Mary couldn't wait to get her installed at Homings on a permanent basis and was already talking excitedly about the three of them going away for a holiday once Sir Gerald was well enough.

Three days before Piers was due back from New York Dulcie arrived at Homings. If there was one person she dreaded meeting almost as much as Piers, it was Piers' mother, but she need not have worried. After she had greeted her sister-in-law Dulcie hugged Selina warmly. 'My dear, I'm so pleased that Gerald's long-lost daughter is you... I can't wait to tell Piers.'

'He already knows.' She said it quietly, aching with the pain of their final confrontation.

Dulcie eyed her speculatively but said nothing.

It wasn't until just after dinner that she said firmly, 'Selina and I are going for a walk in the gardens—alone. It's my turn to get to know her.'

There was no way Selina could refuse. The summer evening was warm without being close.

'I can't tell you how glad we all are to have found you at last, Selina. This will do wonders for Gerald, I know. He's suffered a tremendous burden of guilt over the years.'

'My mother was more to blame really.' She

said it in a low voice. 'I used to hate my father… I thought he'd rejected me… And then I started hating myself… I thought you would all hate me too.'

'Selina no one hates you.'

'Not even Piers?' Selina retorted bitterly.

There was a small silence when she cursed her stupid tongue. Why had she said that?

'I should say especially not my son,' Dulcie said quietly at last. 'He loves you, Selina.'

'Has he *told* you that?' She couldn't bear to look at Dulcie, knowing as she did that the other woman must be wrong.

To her surprise Dulcie responded wryly, 'My dear, I'm his mother. He doesn't need to tell me.'

'I think you're confusing desire with love,' Selina said at last. 'He may want me, but I can't see how he could love me…especially not now…'

'Why don't you ask him?'

Selina could feel her skin change colour. What Dulcie was suggesting was impossible. But what if she was right? What if Piers did love her? How could he, she derided herself? He had never said that he did. Neither did you, a contrary inward voice reminded her…

Dulcie spoke again, her voice calm and assured. 'Ask him Selina,' she told her. 'Or isn't the answer important enough for you to find out?'

Her small sound of pain must have betrayed her because Dulcie continued softly. 'It's not for me to say of course, but sometimes it's worth taking a risk for the important things in life.'

'If he does love me why doesn't he…'

'Tell you? According to Mary the two of you had a quarrel before he left for New York. He's a very proud man Selina, and if you've given him reason to believe you don't care about him, he's hardly likely to tell you what he feels.'

'He despises me.' The words burst out of her. 'He despises me and hates me as he did my mother… I know, I saw his face when I told him who I was.' Her anguish must have reached the other woman because she sighed and said softly.

'My dear, have you thought that he also loves and respects your father… Personally I believe that every child is itself, not a clone of its parents, but if you will persist in believing that Piers sees you only as the child of your mother, remember that you are also the child of your father too, and much more I would say than you were hers.

Courage, Selina,' she added softly. 'Surely it's better to find out now exactly what his feelings are than to torture yourself as you are doing at the moment?'

If she was torturing herself it was because of the hurtful things she had said to Piers before he left. And he had believed them. Surely if he had really loved her he would have known... She sighed and walked back to the house in silence with her companion.

Nothing more was said on the subject of Piers, but he was never out of her thoughts. On the morning he was due to fly back from New York she wandered tensely through the garden, aching for the sight and touch of him and yet dreading any further confrontation. What would his reaction be when he discovered how easily his family had accepted her? Could their acceptance of her cause a rift between them and him? Perhaps if she went to see him and offered to remove herself from their lives if he should wish it...

She knew she was looking for excuses to see him...but she did not have the courage to simply breeze back into his life and ask him if he loved her. The more she thought about it, the more outrageous the possibility seemed. He had never once given her any indication that he might do so. Gerald, and Dulcie too, to some extent, saw her through rose-coloured glasses... not as Piers saw her.

She was just about to walk back into the house when Dulcie found her. 'Here is my key for Piers' apartment,' she told her softly, 'and this is the address... He should be back sometime this afternoon. I've done all I'm prepared to do Selina...the rest must be up to you.'

All morning she agonised over what she ought to do, but in the end the compulsion to see him proved stronger than anything else. Showering and changing into a cool cotton dress with a matching jacket she rang for a taxi.

Gerald expressed mild surprise when she explained that she was going up to London for the day and probably wouldn't be back until late. Mary smiled at her and fussed about the fact that she would be missing lunch, but Dulcie's brief smile of approval warmed her chilled heart.

Four hours later she was bitterly cursing her impetuosity. She had arrived at Piers' apartment just over an hour ago, and had let herself in. It was immaculately tidy, the large sitting room decorated in firmly masculine creams and browns. She hadn't explored any further than that room and the kitchen, not wanting to intrude any further into Piers' privacy than she must.

It was thirst and tension that drove her into the kitchen to make herself a cup of coffee. Piers should have arrived half an hour ago. She had deliberately timed her own arrival to coincide as closely with his as possible, knowing what the ordeal of waiting for him would do to her already over-burdened nervous system.

Of course it was quite possible that the flight might have been delayed. Such things weren't entirely unknown. But what if he didn't come back alone? What if he was going out somewhere? Why, oh why had she come? Her hand shook alarmingly as she poured out her coffee and she had to search round the immaculate kitchen to find a cloth to mop up the small puddle on the work top.

She had just carried her mug back to the sitting room when she heard a key turning in the main door lock. Her stomach churned wildly, a shiver of prehensile dread sliding down her spine. It was impossible for her to move. She could only stand and stare at the door.

It opened abruptly, thrust wide by the powerfully tense movement of Piers' hand. Her first thought was that he looked almost unbearably tired and thinner too. Beneath his tan his face was drawn, and before he masked them for her, his eyes blazed with a curious mixture of emotions as he saw her standing motionless on front of him.

'Well, well,' he said silkily, flinging his coat and case down on to one of the two settees. 'What have we here? Changed your mind about wanting me to pay for the abortion, is that it?'

It was all going dreadfully wrong. In the time they had been apart she had managed to convince herself that their quarrel hadn't been quite so vitriolic as it had been. Now she realised her mistake. She shouldn't have come here. Piers *didn't* love her and anyone who thought he did was living in cloud cuckoo land. He loathed her, despised and hated her.

'No…' Her voice was shaky and thin.

'Then what the hell *are* you doing here?'

'I…' Her throat was bone dry, and she ran her

tongue nervously over her upper lip. God this was worse by far than she had imagined. 'I wanted to tell you that my…that your…that the family want…want me to be part of it…' Heavens, that wasn't what she had meant to say. What was happening to her?

'Oh yes, I've heard all about them killing the fatted calf,' he said nastily. ''emma wrote and told me. Quite a triumph… Has my uncle been told how much it's going to cost him yet…? What price do you place on your affections Selina…?'

'None…there is no price…except that I be loved in return…' Her voice cracked ominously over the admission but Piers appeared not to notice.

'That's a change of heart if ever I heard one,' he derided bitterly. 'Love? You? You're so cold and wrapped up in your own grievances and bitterness, you aren't capable of loving anyone.'

'That's not true.' Her words had cut deep into her emotions and the denial burst from her without conscious thought.

'Isn't it?' He came to stand in front of her, and her heart ached to see the lines of tiredness drawn in deep grooves alongside his mouth as it twisted in bitter contempt.

All at once a terrible need to wipe that look from his face rose up inside her and would not be denied.

'No, it isn't,' she said quietly, 'I love my father…I love Mary…and…and…' her head came up and looked straight at him, 'and I love you Piers.'

The room had gone deadly quiet, so quiet that she could hear the hum of the refrigerator in the kitchen. Dear God…what had she said? It was too late to retract the words now.

'What did you say?'

Her mouth was dry again and she moistened its tense outline with her tongue. 'Don't do that, damn you,' Piers said harshly.

Nervous and confused, she could only stare at him.

'When did you discover this supposed "love" for me?' he mocked coldly. 'Certainly there was no evidence of it the morning I left for New York.'

'I was doing what I thought was best for you.' Her voice was toneless, her body lethargic and weak. She should not have come here, she knew that now. 'I knew how much you despised my mother…you wanted me…you were even prepared to marry me when you knew that…that you had been my first lover. But how could I let you do it, knowing that I would have to tell you the truth and that you'd hate me for it…that you were only marrying me out of a sense of duty…? If you've ever loved anyone yourself you must know what I mean.'

There was anguish and pain in her voice as it trembled over the last words. If he couldn't love her then let there at least be peace and respect between them. She couldn't endure living her life always in the shadow of his contempt.

It was seconds before she could bring herself to look at him, and when she did she was shocked by the pallor of his skin. She reached out towards him instinctively, thinking he must be ill, her skin turning dark red as he flinched back from her as though unable to endure her touch.

'Dear God,' he said at last. 'Is this *true*? Do you honestly believe it matters a damn to me who your parents are?'

He saw her face, whitening under the cruelty of what he was saying. Of course he didn't care who she was; he didn't care full stop, and yet suddenly she was in his arms, his fingers biting into her waist as he pulled her hard against him, his face buried in the softness of her hair.

'Selina, Selina, don't you realise I'm so deeply in love with you that nothing else matters... nothing...' he told her emphatically, lifting his hands to cup her face, holding her so that she was forced to meet his eyes. 'You little fool...why did you put us both through this hell?'

His mouth on hers unleashed a wild torrent of emotions that made her weak with the aching need to be part of him. Her hands moved feverishly beneath his jacket, impatient of the thin silk of his shirt, her mouth surrendering to the deeply possessive passion of his kiss. He released her slowly, holding her slightly away from him.

'I love you,' he told her softly. 'So much that not another damn thing in the world matters. When I discovered that I was your first lover I felt sure you must feel something for me. I was wild to make sure of you...to tie you to me...I could make you love me I told myself...the ingredients were there.'

'But you kept on saying you didn't trust me... that...'

'What man ever trusts the first woman to make him fall in love,' Piers said dryly. 'Of course I was suspicious of you. You behaved in a suspicious fashion. All those qualifications for an extremely mundane job…the fact that you didn't fall into my bed the first time I looked at you…' He smiled a little then, 'Vain, aren't I? You recoiled from me so intensely the first time I kissed you that I knew that touching you was the one sure way to provoke a reaction from you, and I wanted that reaction. You challenged me but what I hadn't bargained for was my own reaction to you. I was furious, both with myself and with you… Every instinct I possessed told me you were hiding something. I owed it to my own intuition to find out what it was, but when you looked at me with those bruised, vulnerable eyes, all I really wanted to do was to take you in my arms.'

'But you didn't?'

'No, I told myself it was just simply that you were a better actress than I'd suspected. I fought hard against loving you…as every man does. I told myself it was fruitless to even think of loving a woman I couldn't trust, and one moreover who didn't love me in return.'

'I did, but I daren't let you see it. I thought you would hate me because of my mother.'

He gave her a little shake. 'Forget your

mother,' he told her curtly. 'You are yourself, Selina. I know what happened in the past hurt you…but there's no need for you to carry any burden of guilt for what happened. You were innocent…a victim if you like.'

'But you were so angry when I told you.'

'Because of the way you told me,' he corrected wryly, 'plus the fact that I thought you'd simply been using me to get closer to Gerald. That hurt,' he told her simply. 'And when you told me you intended to abort any child you might have conceived.'

'I didn't mean it…'

'Don't you think I don't know that?' He whispered the words fiercely against her skin. 'I can't make it up to you for all you suffered as a child, Selina, but I do love you.'

'The citadel has finally crumbled,' she managed to tease.

'With devastating swiftness. If I'd ever thought that once I possessed you, I'd stop wanting you, these last few days have been enough to prove how wrong I was. There hasn't been a single night when I haven't wanted to wake up and find you in my arms…when my body hasn't ached for yours…when I haven't cursed myself a thousand times for losing my temper and walking out instead of staying… Stay here with me tonight.'

'Mary is expecting me back,' she demurred, her eyes already darkening as she thought of his lean body against her own.

'Then I'll just have to ring her and tell her not to expect you, won't I?' He bent to kiss her throat and Selina surrendered herself to the heady pleasure of his touch, tensing a little when he raised his head and laughed.

'What's wrong?'

'I've just wondered how Uncle Gerald will approach taking me to task for seducing his daughter. No doubt he'll expect me to make an honest woman out of you…'

'And…' Selina queried, mock angrily.

'And I shall of course have to comply,' Piers responded mock virtuously, adding thoughtfully, 'you know if I'd known the truth earlier I could have saved myself a good deal of trouble, couldn't I? All I would have needed to do then to get you to agree to be my wife would have been to make love to you. Gerald would have insisted on our being married.' He sounded so smug that Selina had to laugh.

'And seducing me would have been easy would it?'

His eyes darkened as his glance slid over her body. 'Not easy perhaps,' he said huskily at last, 'but infinitely, infinitely pleasurable.'

As he took her back in his arms, Selina gave a mental 'Thank you' to Dulcie. Without her encouragement she would have not been here today… She stiffened and Piers released her reluctantly. 'If I hadn't come here…would you…'

'Would I have what?' he muttered throatily, busily exploring the delicate convolutions of her ear with his tongue.

'Would you have come to me?'

'Eventually…when my need had overcome my pride. No man likes being rejected the way you rejected me. I needed to see you here today…to hear you saying you love me. I would have come to you, but perhaps I would always have had doubts that my feelings were stronger than yours…and like you I should have found that an intolerable burden to bear. Like any other human being I need to be shown that I'm loved and desired.'

She trembled beneath his regard, her insides melting with need. 'What time is it in New York?' she murmured huskily.

Piers frowned, 'Why?'

'I was just wondering if the time difference meant that you should be in bed. I'd hate to see you suffering from jet lag,' she added mock solicitously, her heart doing crazy things as she saw the way he was looking at her, the naked hunger in his eyes making her shiver in apprehensive delight.

'Right now I'm suffering from something far more acute than jet lag,' he muttered throatily against her skin, 'and the cure for it is a considerable amount of time spent with you in my arms. Starting right now…'

It was over an hour later when Selina heard the phone ring, its insistent peal making her move sleepily away from the warmth of Piers' body. In sleep he looked so much younger, his dark hair ruffled, his mouth relaxed. She trembled slightly, remembering the fierce hunger of his lovemaking and her own abandoned response to it. As she tried to slide out of the bed, Piers reached for her. 'Stay here,' he demanded huskily.

'The phone's ringing,' she protested.

With a faint sigh Piers threw back the bed-clothes, the early evening sun through the blinds striking barred patterns against his skin. She could watch him for hours Selina thought dreamily, her body already tingling alive as she gazed on the male perfection of his. He walked into the sitting room without bothering about a robe. Selina heard him speak as he picked up the receiver. 'Yes, mother she's here…' she heard him say as she slid from the bed to join him. As she approached he stretched out an arm, tethering her against him, her head resting against his chest as he added, 'You can tell Mary she'd better prepare herself for a wedding.' There was a brief silence and then he laughed. 'You'll have to wait a little while for that,' she heard him say, 'but I promise you I'll do my best.'

'What did she say?' Selina asked curiously when he had replaced the receiver.

'Oh nothing much.' Humour glinted in his eyes, quickly changing to desire as he ran his hand along her side, cupping her breast and bending to kiss her. Her mouth flowered under his, the kiss long and sweet. When Piers released her he said teasingly. 'She just wanted to tell me not to be too tardy in providing her with grand-children. I told her I'd do my best… What do you say to us getting in a little practise?'

'I'd say that practise is only needed to make perfect,' Selina responded demurely, 'and you're already that…'

'Well, yes…' he pretended to agree with her, 'but there's always room for a little improvement.'

She was laughing when he picked her up and carried her back to bed…her laughter quickly turning to soft gasps of pleasure as he proceeded to demonstrate the truth of his comment… She must remember to invite the Judge and his wife to the wedding, Selina thought hazily, before the ability to think completely deserted her. After all, if it hadn't been for them…

millsandboon.co.uk Community

Join Us!

The Community is the perfect place to meet and chat to kindred spirits who love books and reading as much as you do, but it's also the place to:

- **Get the inside scoop from authors about their latest books**
- **Learn how to write a romance book with advice from our editors**
- **Help us to continue publishing the best in women's fiction**
- **Share your thoughts on the books we publish**
- **Befriend other users**

Forums: Interact with each other as well as authors, editors and a whole host of other users worldwide.

Blogs: Every registered community member has their own blog to tell the world what they're up to and what's on their mind.

Book Challenge: We're aiming to read 5,000 books and have joined forces with The Reading Agency in our inaugural Book Challenge.

Profile Page: Showcase yourself and keep a record of your recent community activity.

Social Networking: We've added buttons at the end of every post to share via digg, Facebook, Google, Yahoo, technorati and de.licio.us.

www.millsandboon.co.uk